**"They had a proposition for me,"
Rafe said. "One they tried to make
very difficult to refuse."**

She frowned. "What kind of proposition?"

"They wanted me to use our past to try to
get on your good side and convince you to
cooperate."

Her eyes hardened. "And did you agree to this?"

"No," Rafe said forcefully. "Of course not. I
would never do anything to put you or Chloe in
danger."

They let that hang in the air for a moment, then
she laced her fingers through his and squeezed.
"You don't know how much I've missed you, Rafe.
How many times I've cursed myself for letting
you go."

"You don't think I feel the same?"

Her eyes looked hopeful. "Do you?"

ALANA MATTHEWS

INTERNAL AFFAIRS

HARLEQUIN®
entertain, enrich, inspire™

Recycling programs
for this product may
not exist in your area.

ISBN-13: 978-0-373-74720-7

INTERNAL AFFAIRS

Copyright © 2013 by Alana Matthews

www.Harlequin.com

Printed in U.S.A.

ABOUT THE AUTHOR

Alana Matthews can't remember a time when she didn't want to be a writer. As a child, she was a permanent fixture in her local library, and she soon turned her passion for books into writing short stories, and finally novels. A longtime fan of romantic suspense, Alana felt she had no choice but to try her hand at the genre, and she is thrilled to be writing for Harlequin Intrigue. Alana makes her home in a small town near the coast of Southern California, where she spends her time writing, composing music and watching her favorite movies.

Send a message to Alana at her website, www.alanamatthews.com.

Books by Alana Matthews

HARLEQUIN INTRIGUE
1208—MAN UNDERCOVER
1239—BODY ARMOR
1271—WATERFORD POINT
1339—A WANTED MAN
1399—INTERNAL AFFAIRS

CAST OF CHARACTERS

Lisa Tobin—A divorced single mother trying to adjust to her new life in St. Louis while dealing with an ex-husband who won't take no for an answer.

Rafe Franco—A sheriff's deputy from a family of cops who is anxious for a promotion but struggling to live up to the family name.

Oliver Sloan—Lisa's obsessive ex-husband. A prominent businessman who secretly runs a crime syndicate.

Kate Franco—Rafe's sister, a no-nonsense sheriff's homicide detective whom Rafe has always looked up to.

Chloe—Lisa's beautiful three-year-old daughter, who is wise beyond her years.

Grandma Natalie—Rafe and Kate's grandmother, who welcomes Lisa and Chloe into her home with open arms.

Bea Turner—Lisa's housekeeper, who wields a mean shotgun and knows how to use it.

Chapter One

She opened her eyes with a start, not sure what had awakened her.

She was alone in the room, which was quiet except for the sound of an autumn breeze outside her window and the faint metallic squeak of the bed springs.

Had it been Chloe?

Squinting at the clock—which read 4:32 a.m.—she stilled herself and listened carefully, using the supersonic hearing only a mother possesses, tuning it in to Chloe's frequency.

But she heard nothing.

No whimpering. No cries in the night.

Even as a baby, Chloe had been a sound sleeper. And now that she was just past her third year, she was nearly impossible to get out of bed in the morning. The girl liked her rest and, unlike her mother, could snooze through a thunderstorm.

But what Lisa Tobin had heard was not thunder.

The noise, if she hadn't dreamed it—and she didn't think she had—was high-pitched and abrasive. Like glass shattering.

A window?

Was there an intruder in the house?

Icy dread sluiced through her bloodstream as the thought took hold. She listened awhile longer, hoping it was just her overactive imagination, and the moment she convinced herself it *was,* she heard another sound—a faint, muffled crash—coming from downstairs.

Definitely *not* her imagination.

There was someone down there.

Could it be Beatrice? Had she awakened in the middle of the night and decided to get an early start on her housekeeping?

Not likely. Bea was efficient, but she wasn't overly ambitious and was as sound a sleeper as Chloe. And even if she *were* tidying up, she had never been the clumsy type. The woman was as stealthy as an alley cat.

So intruder it was. Probably that punk kid from next door trying to prove himself to his punk buddies.

There had been a rash of break-ins up and down the street in the past few weeks and everyone pretty much suspected the kid. He was the product of a broken home—something Lisa was all too familiar with—and had been acting out ever since he'd reached puberty. In the year and a half she had lived in this house, the boy had been arrested three times. Twice for drugs, and once for burglary. And he was undoubtedly working his way toward arrest number four.

So what should she do?

Sit here and let him clean the place out?

Lisa's first instinct was to call the police, but as she reached to the nightstand for her cell phone, she remembered that she had left it in her purse, which was sitting on the table in the foyer downstairs. She had never had a landline installed, and now cursed herself for it.

So she had two choices. Stay put and hope the punk didn't work his way up the stairs…

Or confront him.

Neither choice thrilled Lisa, but she was not the shrinking-violet type and she wasn't about to sit here, waiting to be victimized.

So option number two it was.

Throwing her blankets aside, she sat up, swung her legs over the side of the bed, then got to her feet and pulled her robe on. She would need protection, of course. You don't go into a situation like this without it.

But what kind of protection?

A gun?

Lisa didn't like guns. Hated them, in fact. Had only held one in her hands twice in her lifetime and had felt extremely uncomfortable each time. But before he moved out, her ex-husband, Oliver, had insisted on putting a pistol in a lockbox on the hall closet shelf, telling her not to hesitate to use it if necessary.

It was a typical Oliver move. He was no stranger to violence—something she had learned only in the last days of their marriage, and part of the reason she had filed for a divorce. His stubborn refusal to consider her feelings—the pistol, for example—was the other part. She had thought she was marrying a prince charming but quickly discovered that there was something deadly beneath that charm. Something dangerous and controlling.

And intimidating.

A Dr. Jekyll who had quickly morphed into Mr. Hyde.

But Lisa had never been turned on by bad boys. She had too much self-respect for that. And where she had once felt warmth, she now felt trepidation whenever she encountered him. An uneasiness that wormed its way into her gut every time she saw him.

As much as she hated to admit it, however, Oliver had been right about the gun. And despite the punk's young age, confronting him without a weapon would be foolhardy.

She didn't have to use it, of course. Merely wave it at him to scare him away. Get to her cell phone and call the cops.

So that was the plan.

One she desperately hoped wouldn't go awry.

Sucking in a deep breath, she moved to her bedroom door and opened it a crack, peering out into the dark stillness of the second-floor hallway.

Empty.

Steeling herself, she stepped into that stillness and quickly made her way to Chloe's bedroom. She wasn't about to confront *anyone* without first checking to see that her little girl was safe.

She carefully turned the knob and pushed the door open. To her relief, Chloe was wrapped in her blankets, her tiny figure illuminated by the moonlight from the window, her shallow chest rising and falling.

Despite her trepidation, Lisa felt a sudden

warmth spread inside her. The sight of Chloe sleeping always had that effect on her. It had been a lousy couple of years, yet Chloe had been the one constant, the one shining star, in Lisa's universe.

Reassured that her daughter was safe, she clicked the lock button, then pulled the door shut. She didn't like the idea of locking Chloe in, but didn't want to take any chances, either.

Turning now, she headed back down the hallway toward the stairs, stopping at the narrow closet on the left side of the landing.

Checking the darkness at the bottom of the stairs, she quietly opened the closet door, reached to the overhead shelf and found the wooden box where Oliver had left it, almost a year ago. It was secured by a small lock with a combination that was easy enough to remember: Chloe's birth date.

Dialing it in, Lisa unfastened the lock, opened the box, then carefully removed the loaded pistol. She didn't feel comfortable hefting it, but what choice did she have?

"Just point it and shoot," Oliver had told her during one of his more generous moments. "That's all you have to remember."

Easier said than done, she thought.

Returning the box to the shelf, she closed

the closet door and turned again toward the mouth of the stairs, listening for more sounds from below.

It was eerily silent now.

No rummaging noises, no whispering voices—assuming there was more than one intruder—no footsteps…

Nothing.

Lisa had all but come to the conclusion that the burglar had left when she heard it: the faint, almost imperceptible clink of a glass and the sound of pouring liquid.

Someone was still down there all right—but whoever it was wasn't ransacking her house. He was helping himself to a drink from the wet bar.

What the heck?

Lowering the pistol to her side, Lisa started down the stairs, her heart thumping with every step. She was barefoot, but like the stairways in many old St. Louis homes, this one was made of wood and was full of creaks and groans, the carpet covering it doing little to muffle the sound of her descent. She may as well have announced her entrance with the trill of trumpets.

As she reached the living room, clutching the gun tightly at her side, a lamp next to the sofa came to life, startling her. She was about to swing the gun upward when she stopped herself, realizing who it was.

Oliver. Drunk or stoned, as usual, sitting on the sofa with his feet up on the coffee table, a glass of vodka in hand.

"You've gotta work on your stealth skills, babe. I could hear you at the top of the stairs."

As her heartbeat slowed, anger rose in Lisa's chest, crowding out the fear she was already feeling. "I almost shot you, Oliver. What the heck are you doing here?"

She glanced around the room and saw what had made the noise that got her out of bed: a picture frame lay on the polished wooden floorboards, its glass shattered. The photo inside was one she had always loved—she and Chloe in front of the lake house, Chloe squirming happily in her arms. It had been taken at a better time in her marriage, nearly two years ago, before Oliver had released Mr. Hyde from his cage.

She had no idea if he had purposely knocked it from the end table or had merely stumbled into it. Whatever the cause, she'd now have to clean up the mess and replace the frame. Another black mark in a string of them as far as Oliver was concerned.

He didn't answer her question immediately. Instead, he took a sip of his vodka and gave her a long, slow smile.

"What's the matter, Leese, you don't like me darkening your doorstep? This is, after all, *my* house."

"Tell that to my attorney."

"Ah," he said, "your attorney. I'll bet you'd love to have a reason to give him a call. Real movie-star material, that guy."

"I hadn't noticed."

"Uh-huh. Sure. The two of you probably had this planned from the very beginning."

"Had what planned? What are you talking about?"

Oliver smirked, but there was a coldness in his eyes that frightened her. How could she not have known that he was a sociopath when she met him? How could she have let him seduce her into believing he was her man on a white horse?

"I've been thinking about this ever since you tricked me into the divorce," he said.

"Tricked you?"

"What else would you call it?"

"Surviving," she said, then sighed. "It's been nearly a year, Oliver. Time to move on."

"You and your pretty-boy lawyer planned

this, didn't you? You knew I was a rich, successful businessman and you targeted me, roped me in, used that cute little rear of yours to break me down, take advantage of me. Started snooping around behind my back, sticking your nose in things you had no right getting into."

She thought about Harvey, her handsome but overly earnest attorney who was nearly twice her age, married and had three kids. Their relationship had always been strictly professional.

"You're insane."

"Am I? You got your hooks in me good, babe. I take one look at you in that robe, I get as a randy as a teenager."

Lisa felt her dinner backing up on her. The thought that she'd ever had the desire to take this man to bed gave her an urgent need for a box of gingersnaps. Or a chug of Pepto Bismol.

"Don't flatter yourself," she told him.

"I was *trying* to flatter *you*."

She stared at him. "Get out of here, Oliver. You don't live here anymore, and you know what's at stake. So go home."

"And what if I don't?" He shifted his gaze

to the gun at her side. "You gonna put a hole in me?"

She frowned at him, then moved to the long table against the wall and set down the gun down, glad to be rid of it.

As she stepped away, she said, "You can take it with you, as far as I'm concerned. I don't ever want you thinking I owe you any favors."

The coldness filled his entire face now as he swung his feet off the table and stood up. "Let's talk about favors, why don't we?"

He moved toward her, and Lisa found herself backing away slightly, wondering now if she should have been so quick to put down the gun. Oliver carried with him such a sense of menace that she was unsure of what he might do.

Despite his history of violence, however, he had never threatened either her or Chloe and she hoped that would continue to hold true.

"You weren't so anxious to refuse my favors when I got you out of that dump of an apartment you lived in. I didn't see you protesting when I put you in a brand-new Volvo. Made sure you and Chloe had all those pretty little clothes to wear."

"I've never said I'm not grateful, Oliver, but

none of that means you own me. And right now you're trespassing."

He moved in close, trapping her against the wall. "Trespassing? I haven't been around here in months and this is how you treat me?"

Lisa's heart started thumping again. "Get out of here, now, or I swear I'll—"

It came suddenly and without warning. Oliver's hand shot toward her, grabbing her by the throat, slamming her roughly against the wall.

Lisa struggled, feeling her air cut off. She tried to speak but couldn't.

"I'm sorry," Oliver said. "What was that? Were you about to threaten me again? Tell me I don't have the right to come into a house I bought and paid for? You think some computer file you've got stashed, or some piece of paper your lawyer drafted up is gonna change that?"

Panic rose in Lisa's chest. She could barely breathe.

Upstairs, Chloe started to cry, the sound muffled by her door. But Lisa doubted it was their voices that had awakened her. Her usual sound sleep had instead been disturbed by that sense of menace that Oliver carried with him wherever he went. A malignant contagion stirring the air around them.

As Lisa struggled to breathe, he loosened his grip on her throat and she stumbled sideways. But before she could move away from him, he grabbed hold of her arm and shoved her back against the wall.

She was too stunned to move. This was the first time he had ever laid a hand on her.

"Don't you talk to me like that again, you little gold digger." He held her in place and slipped his free hand inside her robe, grabbing her right breast, rubbing his thumb over her nipple. "You may have snagged the gold, but the way I see it, you've got a long way to go before you earn—"

A ratcheting sound cut him off. They turned and saw Beatrice standing at the foot of the stairs, a shotgun in her hands, leveled at Oliver.

"You'd best get your paws off her real quick, son. I wouldn't want to muss up the lady's new robe."

Tears of relief filled Lisa's eyes. She hadn't even known Bea *owned* a shotgun—wouldn't have approved if she did, not with Chloe in the house—but the old woman looked as if she knew how to use it and Lisa welcomed the sight.

"If you think I'm kidding," Bea continued, "just try me."

Oliver released Lisa, but his body went rigid, the coldness in his eyes turning into a hard, angry stare. "You don't have the guts, you old bat."

"Don't I?" She moved forward. "My daddy taught me how to use this scattergun when I was twelve years old. I've never shot at nothin' but tin cans, but I'm all too happy to find out what a round of buck can do to a grown man's face. I don't imagine it'll be pretty."

"I didn't come here alone," Oliver told her. "I've got men outside and all I have to do is sound the alarm."

Bea smiled. "You go right ahead and do that, son, see what it gets you."

He studied her a moment longer, then did as she asked and backed away, throwing his hands up as he moved. "Never argue with a shotgun."

"Damn right."

Lisa took a deep breath and said, "Get out of here, Oliver, and don't come back."

He snapped his gaze toward her. "Or what?"

"Or I go to the police."

"Why? Because I copped a feel?" He grinned. "Judging by the way your body reacted, I'd say you were enjoying it."

"You know what I'm talking about," Lisa said.

His face got hard and Bea gestured with the shotgun. "Son, I'm about two tics away from squeezing this trigger—and it isn't much of a target, but I'll be aiming at your talliwacker."

Oliver's eyes narrowed. "You're gonna regret this," he said, then looked at Lisa. "Both of you."

He walked to the front door and yanked it open, then turned in the doorway and smiled at them again, using his thumb and forefinger to form a gun.

"You're about to find out what happens to women who dump on Oliver Sloan…"

He pretended to pull the trigger, then turned again and went outside.

Chapter Two

The call came in two hours earlier. Gunshots heard by an insomniac, coming from the auto repair shop next to his apartment building.

"Unit Fourteen, we've got a possible 142 in progress, can you respond?"

"Roger, dispatch. I'm on it."

Sheriff's deputy Rafael Franco was in the middle of his usual graveyard shift, happy to have the distraction after a night of shoveling up street drunks and carting them to the holding tank. It was a part of the job he had never enjoyed, mostly because his skill and brains were being underutilized by the department.

His college diploma still had a bit of wet ink on it, but he was frustrated that he hadn't yet been promoted.

Rafe had been with the Sheriff's department for nearly three years now, the newest and greenest member of the Franco family to wear a badge. The Francos and law enforcement went all the way back to his great-great-grandfather Tomas, an Italian immigrant who had joined the St. Louis police force when it was little more than a ragtag group of men with guns and good intentions.

Rafe knew he had a lot to live up to, but he felt restless working the streets, and figured he had already paid his dues. He was tired of patrol duty. What he really wanted was to join his sister, Kate, on the homicide squad, where brains and reasoning and solid evidence-gathering far outweighed your ability to heft a drunk into the backseat of your cruiser.

Unfortunately, Rafe didn't get the impression he'd be bumped up anytime soon. But a report of gunshots gave him hope. Not that he wished any other human being ill, but if he happened to luck into something big, maybe he'd get a chance to demonstrate his investigative skills.

He also didn't mind the distraction from his thoughts tonight. As always, he had taken a long nap before reporting to duty, and a dream he'd had was haunting him—a vague, half-remembered remnant from his college years, featuring a girl he had once loved. He had awakened from it feeling disoriented and a little sad, filled with a vague, undefinable yearning that he couldn't quite shake.

Rafe hadn't seen the girl in over three years now, but she still showed up on the doorstep of his mind every now and then and he'd often thought of trying to contact her. Their breakup had been mutual—both convinced that they were too young to be getting serious—but Rafe often regretted the decision and wondered if she did, too.

He hadn't met a woman since who had made him feel the way she had. And that dream, as hazy as it was, hadn't done him any favors.

THE AUTO BODY SHOP was located on a deserted city street, nestled between a run-down apartment building and an abandoned drive-in liquor store.

The place was dark when Rafe pulled up to the curb. A sea of cars in various states of disrepair crowded the lot out front, making the place look more like a junkyard than a body shop. The garage—a large rectangular structure—was located in back and, by Rafe's count, sported nine repair bays, each with its aluminum roll door closed and locked for the night.

Off to the right of the building was a connecting office with its front door hanging open, nothing but darkness beyond.

Something obviously wasn't right here.

To Rafe's mind, this was an indication that the caller might not have been hearing things. Too often reports of gunshots are nothing more than a car backfiring or kids playing with firecrackers, but that open door suggested something far more sinister.

Rafe called it in, told the dispatcher he was on the scene. That he'd stay in radio contact as he checked it out.

Grabbing his flashlight from the glove compartment, he killed his engine and climbed out of the cruiser. He moved off to his left, not wanting to approach the open door directly, in case the shooter—assuming there was one—was still inside.

Stepping into the sea of cars, he stayed low and carefully made his way around and through them, drawing closer to the office, making sure to come at the doorway from an angle.

He was about ten yards away when he stopped, crouched behind an old Chevy Malibu missing its grill, and peered into the darkness beyond the threshold, looking for signs of life inside.

Nothing but still air in there.

Nobody home.

Satisfied that he was alone out here, Rafe stood up, clicked the radio on his shoulder.

"Dispatch, this is Unit Fourteen. Looks like it's clear out here, but I'm headed inside for a closer look."

"Do you need backup?"

"I think I'm good for now," Rafe said. "I'll stay in radio contact."

"Roger, Fourteen."

Switching the flashlight on, Rafe pointed it toward the building, then dropped a hand to the holster on his hip and unsnapped it, resting his palm against the grip of his Glock.

Using the beam to guide him, he approached the doorway and stepped through it, finding nothing but your typical cluttered office—a desk piled with paperwork, an adding machine, a few metal chairs, a bookshelf full of repair manuals, an old computer. There was a faded calendar on the wall featuring the *Motor Babe of the Month* wearing a barely there bikini and holding a wrench provocatively as she posed in front of a souped-up Ford Mustang.

Off to the left was another doorway that opened into a garage bathed in moonlight, which filtered in from a bank of high windows. It was about half the size of a football field, and there were cars parked in each of the nine bays, all but one in various states of disassembly.

Rafe smelled the odor of a cooling engine and ran the flashlight beam over the car closest to him—a shiny Jaguar XJ that looked as if it was in fine condition, no body work needed. There was a thin layer of road dust covering it and it didn't seem to have been repaired at any time in the recent past.

So why was it parked in here?

Was it the owner's car?

And, if so, where was he?

Before Rafe could ponder these questions, the beam of his flashlight caught something dark and glistening on the cement directly beneath the Jaguar's front passenger side—

A small pool of red liquid that looked very much like blood.

It was coming from the crack beneath the door.

Rafe's body tensed. Drawing his Glock from its holster, he shone his light through the car window and saw two figures slumped inside, both male, both very dead. Eyes wide. Mouths agape. Judging by their appearance— unshaven, rumpled clothes, with matching bullet holes adorning the middle of their foreheads—they weren't Sunday school teachers.

And this was definitely the work of a professional.

Rafe was about to call it in when he heard a sound coming from across the garage—the faint clang and scrape of metal against concrete, as if someone had accidentally kicked a stray hubcap.

He wasn't alone in here.

Jerking his flashlight beam toward the source of the sound, he illuminated the far end of the garage.

"Sheriff's department," he called out. "Show yourself and take it slow, hands in the air."

He caught a glimpse of movement and reacted instinctively, diving sideways, just as a muzzle flashed and the bark of gunfire filled his ears. One of the Jaguar's side mirrors exploded above his head and he dove for cover behind a tall, rolling tool cabinet.

Dropping the flashlight, he reached for the radio on his shoulder and clicked it on.

"Dispatch, this is Unit Fourteen. I'm under fire. Repeat, I'm under fire."

"Roger, Fourteen, we're sending backup."

More gunshots punched holes in the Jaguar and the tool cabinet, landing way too close for comfort. Rafe quickly snatched up the flashlight and closed it, tucking it into its loop on his belt.

No point in giving this guy a target.

He returned fire—once, twice—then retreated into the darkness behind him and waited.

The gunfire stopped, followed by the longest stretch of silence that Rafe had ever experienced. His heart pounded wildly as he waited for the perp to make a move. He figured the guy would either start shooting again—assuming he had the rounds—or make like a jackrabbit.

Rafe didn't have to wait long for the perp to decide. A dark figure popped up from behind the equally dark silhouette of a car and took off, heading for a door on the left side of the garage.

Rafe shot to his feet and shouted, "Hold it!" as he took off after the guy, leaping over stray tools and car parts that lay on the garage floor.

A moment later he was at the door and about

to crash through it, when he stopped himself, thinking that might not be a wise move.

What if the perp was out there waiting for him?

Instead, he stepped to the right side of the doorway and crouched down to avoid being in the line of fire. Then he reached a hand out, turned the knob, and flung the door open.

As it swung wide, he half expected another flurry of gunshots—

But nothing happened. All he heard was the distant drone of street traffic.

Getting back to his feet, he carefully peeked around the door frame and saw the perp several yards away, working his way through the maze of cars in the front of the lot.

"Police!" Rafe shouted as he took off after him. "Stop right now!"

The guy didn't slow down. He was nearly to the sidewalk now, only feet from where Rafe had left his cruiser. As the perp barreled past the last of the cars, he brought his gun up and shot at the black-and-white, shattering the windshield and puncturing one of the tires.

Rafe swore under his breath and kept running, moving into and through the maze—

Now the guy was on the street and jumping

into a gray BMW. The engine roared to life as Rafe vaulted the hood of a junked Mazda and scrambled after him.

Just as he reached the street, the BMW's rear tires began to spin and smoke, the car laying rubber as it tore away from the curb.

Rafe tried to read the license plate, but the streetlight was too dim and the plate was obscured by darkness. He whirled around, hoping his cruiser was still good to go, and found that the shooter had hit his mark. The right front tire was shredded and leaking air. Fast. No way he'd get very far.

Swearing under his breath again, he watched the BMW disappear down the street, then reached for his radio.

"The suspect has escaped," he said. "He's headed north on Davis Avenue in a gray BMW, license plate unknown. My vehicle has been compromised."

"Roger, Fourteen. Patrol's been alerted and backup is on its way."

AS HE WAITED for his fellow deputies to arrive, Rafe went back into the garage. He found the switch for the overhead lights and took a closer look at the bodies inside the Jaguar.

Two males, approximately thirty years old,

one with a tattoo of a spider on his neck. They both looked Slavic to Rafe, maybe Russian, which immediately brought to mind the Russian mob.

Were these guys connected?

Was it a contract killing?

Judging by the placement of the wounds, Rafe had no doubt it was a professional hit, but he'd failed to get a look at the shooter and had no idea if he'd been chasing another Russian or someone else entirely.

Knowing full well that he was breaking protocol, Rafe untucked and used his shirttail for protection as he reached for the passenger door handle. He'd have a heck of a time explaining any stray prints. Swinging the door open, he leaned inside and carefully checked the pockets of the victim closest to him.

Nothing. No wallet. Keys. Coins. Cigarettes. Not even a stick of gum. Rafe closed the door, then moved around to the driver's side and did the same thing with the other victim, getting the same results. The shooter had obviously cleaned house after he'd made the hit.

Rafe was about to close the car door when he spotted something on the floor mat near the driver's left foot.

A small, narrow slip of paper.

He reached down, snatched it up and tilted it toward the light, noting that it was a receipt for a fill-up at a Western Star service station just across town.

The time stamp read 2:45 a.m.

Rafe knew this could very well be the key to identifying the victims—and, by extension, the shooter. He also knew he should return it to the floor mat where he'd found it. But as the sound of approaching sirens filled his ears, he stuffed it into his jacket pocket and closed the car door.

A moment later, he stepped outside to greet his colleagues.

Chapter Three

"Let's go through it one more time," Kate said.

Rafe balked. "Seriously?"

They were standing outside the auto repair shop. The roll doors had all been raised, the garage overheads lighting the yard as a flurry of crime scene techs moved in and out of the building.

"Look, Rafe, I know it's late, I know your shift is almost over, but if this is a mob hit, things could get sticky. I want to make sure all our bases are covered."

Rafe hadn't been surprised when his big sister, Kate, showed up at the scene. She was the Homicide Squad's best investigator, specializing in organized crime, and anything that smacked of a professional hit was usually passed off to her. She took her job very seriously and had the tenaciousness of a bulldog. She also got results and was the envy of every investigator on the squad.

Growing up in Kate's shadow had not been easy for Rafe. Ever since he'd graduated from college and had joined the department, he had been trying to live up to her reputation. He had put in extra hours, volunteered for event work, even worked the holidays no one else wanted to—all in hopes that he could make just the fraction of the impression that his sister had made. Unfortunately, nobody seemed to have taken notice of these sacrifices.

Including Kate.

"I don't care about working a little overtime," he told her. "I'm here for the duration."

It wasn't as if he could go anywhere anyway. His cruiser was being towed to the police garage as they spoke and he'd have to hitch a ride with one of the other deputies to get back to the station. He was bound to be here at least another hour.

"Good," Kate said. "So let's go through it again."

Rafe sighed. "As I said, I got the call out at about 0300 hours, give or take. Dispatch'll have the exact time."

"And no ID on the caller, right?"

"Right," Rafe said. "Although he said his apartment overlooks the lot."

Kate turned to her partner, a burly guy named Eberhart who stood nearby. Rafe got the feeling the guy had always regarded him as an irritant, and the feeling was mutual.

She signaled to him. "Charlie, get a canvass going on the apartment building. We need eyes on this thing."

Eberhart smirked. "Maybe your little bro here would like to volunteer. He's gotta be good for something."

Kate frowned. "Just get it started, all right?"

Eberhart gave her a salute. "Your wish is my command, O Great Leader." Then he turned and called to a couple of deputies who were huddled near their cruisers. "Look alive, knuckleheads, you've just been recruited."

The guy was a jackass.

When he was gone, Kate returned her attention to Rafe. "Okay, so you responded to the call and arrived at approximately what time?"

"About 3:10. The place was dark, so I notified dispatch and decided to take a look around."

"Did you request backup?"

"We didn't even know for sure that shots

had actually been fired at that point, so I didn't think backup was necessary."

Karen gave him a stony look. "And as a consequence, you almost got your rear end shot off and the suspect got away."

Rafe felt his cheeks go red. As a big sister, Kate had never been much of a nurturer, and it was just like her to point out any mistakes he may have made.

He frowned at her and said, "Are you going to bust my chops or let me talk?"

"Go on."

"When I got close to the building, I saw the door was ajar—"

"And you *still* didn't call for backup?"

Rafe sighed. "What exactly are you investigating here? Me or the murders? I told dispatch what I was doing every step of the way. I'm not exactly a rookie, you know."

Her frequent interruptions and insistence that he repeat his story made *him* feel like a suspect, as if she were expecting to expose him in some kind of lie. But he knew from previous conversations with her that this was merely a technique she employed to try to jog a witness's memory and draw out more details.

"Just tell me what happened when you got inside," she said.

"I saw the Jaguar, the bodies, then the shooting started."

"And where was the suspect?"

"Across the garage." Rafe pointed to the building behind them. "He came out that door and was gone before I could stop him."

"Did you at least get a look at him?"

"My answer hasn't changed since the last time you asked me. It was too dark. And he was wearing a hoodie."

"And no license number from the car he was driving?"

Rafe just gave her a look.

"Okay," she said, reading his unspoken message. She flipped her notebook shut and clipped her pen to it before putting it in her coat pocket. "Enough business for now. How are you doing? It isn't fun getting shot at."

"The only thing that's hurting is my pride," Rafe said. "I wish I could've caught the guy."

"Sounds like you did what you could, little brother. I wouldn't sweat it, if I were you."

"Thanks. What do you want me to do now?"

Kate waved a hand at him. "You're done

here. Find your ride, go back to the station and write up your report."

"That's it?"

Her eyebrows went up. "You have a better idea?"

He shrugged. "I thought I might be able to assist somehow. Maybe help Eberhart with that canvass. Or help you inspect the crime scene." He paused. "I'm thinking the owner of the auto repair shop must be connected to these guys somehow. Otherwise, what were they doing here?"

Kate smiled. "You just can't wait to get rid of that uniform, can you?"

He hadn't realized it was so obvious. The last thing he wanted was to come across like an anxious puppy. At twenty-five, he was still young, but he'd always thought he was pretty mature for his age. Ready to take the next step in his career.

Maybe he'd been deluding himself.

"As I said, I just want to help."

Kate's smile disappeared and she suddenly looked very serious. "You can help by being patient and doing your job, Rafael. Your time will come, but it may not be as soon as you want it to be, and that's something you'll just have to live with."

Spoken like a true big sister, he thought. With just the right amount of condescension. Rafe had the urge to tell her where to stuff it, but remained professional.

"So are we good?" Kate asked.

"We're good," Rafe said.

She turned away and was about to start toward the garage when she stopped. "Just one last question."

"Which is?"

"You didn't touch the car, right? Didn't try to do a little investigating of your own?"

Rafe felt his heart kick up and thought about the gas receipt that was still in his pocket. He'd meant to give it to her, but now he wasn't so sure that was a good idea. Surely they'd be able to identify the bodies through fingerprint analysis, and his breach of protocol would never have to come to light.

If worse came to worst, he could give it to her later, claim he'd found it on the garage floor and in the excitement that followed had forgotten about it. But handing it over now would be a mistake. Especially after she had just treated him like a redheaded stepchild.

"Rafe?"

He blinked at her. "Give me some credit,

sis, I'm not stupid enough to interfere with a crime scene."

"You're sure about that?"

"Yes," he lied. "Absolutely sure."

She studied him skeptically. The woman had always had the uncanny ability to read him. Had caught him in a number of lies as they grew up, but had always been merciful enough not to tell their parents.

Kate was a good six years older than Rafe and that gap had given her enough insight to avoid the pettiness of sibling rivalry. She may not have been a nurturer, but she wasn't a traitor, either. And nobody could ever say that the Franco kids didn't look out for one another.

Even so, she really annoyed him sometimes.

"I'm going to trust you on that," she said. "But if any fingerprints show up, you're on your own."

"They won't," he told her, relieved that he'd had the wherewithal to use his shirttail for protection. "I promise."

She studied him a moment longer, then nodded and walked away, heading into the garage.

When she was gone, Rafe let out a long breath and tried not to feel too guilty.

Chapter Four

"So is your sister seeing anyone these days?"

The deputy he'd snagged to drive him back to the station was a guy named Phil Harris. Harris was what qualified in the patrol division as an old-timer, although he couldn't yet be over forty. He'd been with the department since he was Rafe's age and had never progressed further than a RS-3 pay grade.

Harris was a good cop, but not the most ambitious guy in the department.

"Sorry, Phil, I don't keep track of her love life. You'd have to ask her."

Harris wasn't the first deputy to approach Rafe about Kate. One of the hazards of working in the same department as your sister was that you had to put up with every hot-to-trot single—and sometimes married—guy on the job, looking to get into her pants. Rafe would be the first to admit that Kate was a looker—she *did* have the Franco genes, after all—but the last thing he wanted to think about was who she may or may not be sleeping with.

"I was hoping you'd put in a good word for me," Harris said. "Let her know I'm interested."

What was this—high school?

Rafe shook his head. "First, I've got zero influence over Kate. And second, you might as well stand in line. You're about the fifteenth deputy who's asked me about her in the last month alone—and the competition is stiff."

"How stiff?"

"Like County Undersheriff stiff."

Harris's eyebrows shot up. "You're telling me she's been hitting it with Macon?"

"That's the rumor," Rafe said. "But, as I told you, I don't keep track. I'm having a hard enough time with my own love life."

Harris turned. "I thought you were dating that blonde in dispatch? The one with the big—"

"That's been over for months," Rafe said. "In fact, it was over before it really got started. No chemistry. Besides, I don't have time for romance. I've got to think about my career."

Harris snorted. "You sound like me about twenty years ago. I passed up on a perfectly good relationship—a gal I could have had a life with—all because I thought I didn't have time for that nonsense. Now look at me. I'm alone and going nowhere. And believe me, it isn't much fun."

Rafe found his mind wandering back to last night's dream and the girl he'd left behind. He shook the thought away.

"Boo-hoo," he said. "I'm still not going to set you up with my sister."

Harris grinned. "You saw what I was trying to do there, huh?"

"From a couple hundred yards away."

THEY WEREN'T TWO MILES from the station house when Harris's radio came to life.

"Dispatch to Unit Ten, do you read me?"

Harris snatched up his handset. "This is Ten. What do you got?"

"A possible 273 D in Forest Park. Can you respond?"

Two-seventy-three D was code for a domestic dispute, every deputy's least favorite type of call. Too often it was a husband being abusive to his wife, and Rafe had no tolerance for such men. It took everything he had to keep himself from giving the abuser a very painful life lesson.

Harris turned to him. "You in?"

Rafe was already supposed to be off the clock, but despite his reservations, he found that he still had a lot of pent-up energy coursing through his veins.

"Sure," he said.

Harris clicked the handset. "I'm on it, dispatch. Deputy Franco assisting. Give me the address."

Ten minutes later they pulled into Forest Park, an affluent section of St. Louis, not far from the Hill, where Rafe lived. The neighborhood featured a mix of 2-million and 3-million-dollar homes. Tudors. Dutch colonials. A couple of Cape Cods thrown in for good measure. It was the kind of place that made deputies like Rafe and Harris feel as if they were little more than servants to the rich and powerful.

Rafe had to fight against this feeling as they pulled up to the house in question, a two-story colonial. The front door was nearly the size of his entire apartment.

They got out and he waited as Harris knocked.

A voice on the intercom came to life. "Yes?"

"Sheriff's department," Harris said. "You called us about a domestic dispute?"

A moment later, the door opened and an

elderly woman who was built like a bull terrier, ushered them inside.

"Come in, come in," she said. "The no-good creep is gone, but we want to file a formal complaint against him."

"Against whom?" Rafe asked as they followed her into a large foyer.

"The former man of the house. He broke in through the back door and raised quite a fuss."

"Is anyone hurt?"

"No, but it got pretty dodgy there for a minute."

Rafe nodded. "So who is this guy? Your husband?"

The old woman laughed. "Me? No. I'm just the hired help. But I had to scare him off with my scattergun. Couldn't have him treating Lisa like that."

"Lisa?"

"The lady of the house."

Just as she said this, they stepped into an expansive, tastefully furnished living room and Rafe's heart momentarily seized up as his gaze shifted to the woman sitting on a large white sofa in the center of the room.

The name *Lisa* was not uncommon, but the face that went with it was all too familiar. One that Rafe knew quite well but hadn't seen in over three years.

Except in his dream last night.

Call it fate or luck or serendipity, but the woman sitting on that sofa—the woman holding a sleeping child in her lap—was none other than Lisa Tobin.

His college sweetheart.

Chapter Five

Lisa thought she must be dreaming.

Or simply mistaken.

But one of the deputies Beatrice had just escorted into the living room looked a lot like…

She swallowed, felt her pulse quicken. "Rafe? Rafe Franco?"

He stopped at the edge of the foyer, nearly frozen in place. He looked a little older—especially in that uniform—no longer the boy she had known in college, but a man. A man who had filled out with muscle and angular edges and broader shoulders. A man who had obviously spent the past few years working out and had the body to prove it.

But it was him, all right. It was Rafe.

A new and improved Rafe.

His eyes went wide at the sight of her, his voice tinged with disbelief. "Lisa?"

Lisa's mind suddenly flooded with images

from the past—the pain, the heartbreak she'd felt in those days following their breakup. The sense of loss and confusion and, most of all, fear. Especially when she found out she was…

She stopped short, pulling herself back to the present. She carefully laid Chloe on the sofa and got to her feet, moving to Rafe, who now looked like the proverbial deer caught in the headlights.

She felt pretty much the same way.

"My God," she said, overcome by a kind of surreal numbness. They met in the middle of the room, Rafe pulling her into a hug as Bea and the other deputy looked on in surprise.

Lisa could feel Rafe's taught muscles pressing against her, and it gave her a small thrill to be back in his arms after all this time. It felt different, yet much the same.

His smell hadn't changed. The smell of his hair and his skin and the faint remnants of aftershave…

She reluctantly pulled away from him now, holding him at arm's length, trying to process this unexpected turn of events.

"What are you doing here?" she asked. "How…?"

"I've been living here for a few years now."

"I know your family's from St. Louis, but I thought you went to California after college. All that talk about beaches and surfing and…"

"That lasted about two months before I realized I really don't like sand. So I decided to go into the family business." He gestured. "I tried to get ahold of you when I came back. I even called your mother, but she had no idea where you'd gone."

Not surprising, Lisa thought. She and her mother had never gotten along.

She nodded. "It's a long story. And not worth repeating."

"When did you move to St. Louis?"

"About a year ago. I moved here with…" She hesitated, not wanting to talk about her marriage and divorce. As if talk of Oliver would spoil this moment. "As I said, it's a long story."

Now Rafe's gaze shifted to the sofa, to Chloe, his eyes clouding with confusion. "She can't be yours."

"I'm afraid so," Lisa said, her heart kicking up a notch. "All thirty pounds of her."

"How old is she?"

Lisa hesitated. "She was three last month." She half expected him to start doing the math, but the significance of the timing seemed to be lost on him.

"I guess you were busy while I was pretending to be a beach bum," he said. "I'm happy for you, Leese. She's beautiful."

Because she looks like you, Lisa thought, suddenly overwhelmed by an intense, gut-wrenching guilt.

But this wasn't the proper time and place for confessionals. She wasn't sure if there *was* a proper time and place. Not over three years and another life later. Not when part of her past had been sprung on her without warning or preparation. This was a delicate situation that needed to be dealt with in private—with tact and sensitivity.

Lisa couldn't count the number of times she had wanted to pick up the phone and call Rafe. Tell him that long story in detail. But it was too much to handle right now, too much to process.

So she merely nodded in response and said, "Her name is Chloe."

She saw confusion in Rafe's eyes, and maybe a hint of disappointment, too. Not because of Chloe, but because she had somehow managed to move on with her life in a much bigger way than either of them could have expected back in college. A life that, despite the circumstances, hadn't included Rafe.

But before he could speak again, his partner said, "I hate to interrupt this happy reunion, folks, but we *are* here for a reason." He looked at Lisa. "Do you have a complaint to make?"

Lisa pulled herself from her thoughts and shook her head. "Calling you was Bea's idea. I don't really want to stir up any trouble."

"Oh, for God sakes," Bea said. "The creep broke into your house and started manhandling you."

"What creep?" Rafe asked, looking concerned. "The so-called former man of the house?"

Lisa nodded. "My ex. But it really wasn't that big of a deal. He has a few boundary issues, is all."

Rafe frowned. "Tell me about the manhandling part. Did he hurt you?"

Lisa hesitated. "He…he pawed me a little."

"Pawed you?" Bea cried, turning to Rafe. "He had her up against the wall and was slobbering over her like a Saturday-night sex fiend. And if I'm not mistaken, he had her by the throat at one point. As I told you, if

I hadn't turned my scattergun on him, he'd probably still be here."

Now Rafe's partner stepped toward them. The name above his badge read Harris. "Ma'am, we can't force you to file a complaint, but it sounds to me as if things got pretty nasty here."

Lisa nodded reluctantly. "Maybe."

"And if I know anything about human nature," Harris continued, "this isn't the last you'll see of this creep. Especially if there's a child involved."

Lisa caught herself glancing at Rafe, but said nothing. Rafe, however, took this as a cue to say, "Has he ever hurt you before?"

"No. That's why I'm so hesitant to press charges. He can be violent, but he's never been violent with me. Or Chloe."

"So what changed?"

Lisa shook her head. "I don't know. He was drunk, maybe a little stoned. We've been separated for nearly a year and the divorce became final three months ago. But I was the one who filed and he still hasn't accepted it."

Rafe's brows furrowed. "You couldn't have been together very long."

"Long enough for me to realize what I'd gotten myself into."

"Meaning what?"

"As I said, it's a long story."

Rafe nodded. "You also said he can be violent. What did you mean by that?"

"The people he sometimes associates with are not exactly the nicest people in the world. I told him I didn't want them around the house, but he ignored me."

"That still doesn't explain the violent part."

Lisa hesitated again, not sure how much she should say. But she knew that if *she* didn't tell them, Beatrice would, so she might as well put it out there.

She slunk to the sofa. "He had a girlfriend while we were together. I only found out about her when she wound up in the hospital. A friend of mine works at County and saw him when they brought her in."

"For what?"

"A broken jaw. She had to have it wired shut."

Rafe's brows went up now. "And you think he did that to her?"

"I know he did. He told me as much when I confronted him. Said she was a loudmouthed little witch who didn't know when to shut up." Lisa sighed. "That was the last straw. I filed for divorce less than a week later."

She remembered the look in Oliver's eyes when he'd confessed to her. A look that she could only describe as pride. He had been proud of what he'd done to that poor girl. As if he were the king ape who had punished a disobedient subject.

That's when she realized he was a sociopath.

Filing those divorce papers had been another turning point in Lisa's life, and the moment she did it, she felt liberated. Yet, before then, she hadn't even realized she was a prisoner. She had allowed herself to block out the truth simply because Oliver had provided her and Chloe with a home. A family.

And the illusion of happiness.

When she thought about it now, however, maybe Oliver was right. Maybe she *was* a gold digger.

Rafe said, "I know you, Lisa. You always *did* try to avoid confrontations. But if this guy is starting to get violent with you, you need to press charges and file for a restraining order. Deputy Harris is right. He *will* be back."

"I can handle him," she said.

Bea snorted. "By letting him rub you up like a $2 tart? Seems to me *he* was the one doing all the handling."

Lisa felt her face flush, but said nothing. With Bea, you could always count on the truth, no matter how unflattering it might be.

"I'll tell you what," Rafe said, then moved to the sofa and sat next to her. "You don't have to file charges, but at least give me his name."

"Why?"

"I'll go talk to him. Tell him he needs back off."

"You'd better take my scattergun if you do," Bea said.

"Trust me, I've handled my share of tough guys. Most of the time they're more talk than action, and I'm pretty sure I can convince him to leave Lisa alone." He looked at Chloe, who was still fast asleep. "I assume you have custody?"

The question caught Lisa off guard. "Uh, yeah," she said. "Sole custody."

"Good. Then it shouldn't be a problem. What's your ex-husband's name?"

"Sloan," Bea said. "Oliver Sloan."

And to Lisa's surprise, Rafe and Deputy Harris exchanged a look that told her they'd heard the name before. The shock on their faces was hard to miss.

"Oliver Sloan?" Harris said. "You've got to be kidding me."

"You know him?" she asked.

"Better than I'd like to. There isn't anyone in law enforcement who doesn't. Not in St. Louis."

"I don't understand," she said. "Why?"

"Are you serious?"

"Yes," Lisa said. "Oliver's in real estate. He may have problems and a poor choice of friends, but he's a glorified salesman. Why would the police care about that?"

"Because of what he sells," Rafe told her.

Lisa was bewildered. For all his faults, she'd never thought Oliver was involved in anything that would raise the interest of the police—except maybe a bit of real estate hanky-panky that she was convinced he was trying to pull. There was also the incident with his girlfriend, but the woman had never pressed charges.

"I don't understand."

"It's simple," Rafe said. "Your ex-husband is up to his eyeballs in organized crime."

Chapter Six

Oliver Sloan.

When the name came out of the house-keeper's mouth, Rafe wasn't quite sure he'd heard her right.

Oliver Sloan was a bad man.

A very bad man.

Oliver Sloan was nothing less than the local king of organized crime. Drugs. Prostitution. Extortion. Gambling. If it was a thriving illegal enterprise, Sloan's involvement was a given.

The problem, unfortunately, was proving it. Despite years of trying, neither the Sheriff's department nor the St. Louis police had been able to come up with any evidence against him. Too many crime scenes had been sanitized. Too many witnesses had disappeared. Too many suspects had kept their mouths shut and taken their punishment, refusing to reveal who had given the orders.

Oliver Sloan had somehow managed to stay above it all. Had even presented himself to the public as an altruistic businessman. A real estate mogul. But as Harris had said, everyone in St. Louis law enforcement circles knew he was dirty. As dirty as they come.

What Rafe had a hard time stomaching, however, was that Lisa had not only been involved with the guy, but also had actually been *married* to him. Had a *child* with him.

That was just one surprise too many.

Rafe had been feeling shell-shocked ever since he entered the house and saw Lisa sitting on that sofa. And the thought that Oliver Sloan had sired that child was almost too much to bear.

Rafe remembered what he and Lisa had meant to each other in college and how their breakup was largely due to their inability to commit. Even though it was only a little over three years ago, they had seemed so young then. So immature.

But they'd both done a lot of growing up since then. And apparently Lisa herself hadn't had much trouble committing. Not for a while, at least. She had gone straight from that breakup into the arms Oliver Sloan.

But how could she not know what kind of man he was? Was he that good at hiding it?

"Let me get this straight," Rafe said. "You had no idea your ex-husband was suspected of being part of a crime syndicate?"

Lisa shook her head in dismay. "You must have the wrong Oliver Sloan. I've sat in his office, watched him make deals. If anything mob related was going on, I think I would've noticed."

"His company's a front," Harris said. "But, trust me, you aren't the only one he's snookered. There are a few people on the city council who think he's God, and he's got more connections than the pope."

"I can't believe this," Lisa said.

"Well you'd better start wrapping your head around it, because if this guy's giving you grief, you're in a lot more trouble than you—"

"That's enough, Phil." Rafe approached his partner. "We came here to help Lisa, not scare her half to death."

He turned to the sofa, chastising himself for letting this go on as long as it had. Lisa's expression was a mix of fear and disbelief.

"Look, Lisa, I won't kid you. You're probably making the right move, not pressing charges. But that doesn't mean Sloan won't answer for what he did here tonight."

"You're still going to talk to him?"

"As soon as I get off duty. I don't think a civil conversation will hurt, and I doubt he'll do anything stupid. He's not a stupid man."

Rafe felt Harris's gaze on him, probably wearing a look of disbelief himself. Probably thinking *Rafe* was the stupid one. But Harris had maintained a career as a patrol deputy by playing it safe, and what he thought right now wasn't of much interest to Rafe. He was merely a ride back to the station house.

Lisa got to her feet and approached them, pulling Rafe into another hug. He smelled the familiar scent of lavender and was pleased to know she still used the same perfume. He knew it was an odd thing to remember or be comforted by, but that scent had defined her somehow and smelling it now sent a cascade of memories tumbling through his head.

"Thank you," she said. "But be careful. I don't want you getting hurt because of me."

"Don't worry, I'm not the scrawny kid you knew in college."

She laughed. "Believe me, I noticed."

She squeezed him tighter, then pulled away, her look telling him that she suddenly felt awkward about this whole situation. They both needed to step back for a moment, evaluate this unexpected reunion, then proceed from there.

But Rafe hoped she wouldn't mind if he called her. "Is there a number where I can reach you?"

Their gazes connected for a moment, then Lisa moved to a table along the wall, opened a drawer and scribbled something on a scratch pad. Tearing the top sheet off, she folded it twice and handed it to him.

"My cell," she said. "But whatever you do, don't let Oliver get hold of it. Otherwise, he'll start texting me day and night."

"It's safe with me," Rafe said, then looked across the room at little Chloe, who was stirring on the sofa. She was indeed a beautiful child, a reflection of her mother.

Too bad her father was scum.

Rafe nodded toward the girl and said, "My grandmother always told me that children are God's way of granting us eternal life. You're a lucky woman, Leese. And I'm sure you're a wonderful mother."

She smiled wistfully. "Thank you, Rafe."

He gestured to Harris and they went back into the foyer. And as he turned at the front doorway for one last look at the girl he had once loved, he thought he saw tears in her eyes.

"ARE YOU OUTTA YOUR MIND, Franco?" The words flew out of Harris's mouth before he even had the cruiser's engine started. "You think you're just going to walk up to Oliver Sloan and tell him what's what?"

Rafe shrugged. "You have any better ideas?"

"Damn straight I do. Walk away and leave it alone. There's a reason we've never been able to pop this guy. Rumor has it he's even got the *mayor* in his pocket."

"I've never been big on rumors," Rafe said.

"Well, I hope you aren't too big on your job, either, because this guy can ruin your career with a snap of his fingers."

Rafe chuckled. "You watch too many crime shows."

"What I watch is my back, and you'd better watch yours, too. But if you *are* stupid enough to confront this clown, leave my name out of it. I don't need him knowing I'm alive."

Rafe wasn't surprised by Harris's lack of internal fortitude, but it grated on him nevertheless. "Come on, Phil, are you a cop or a glorified Girl Scout?"

"I'm a guy who knows his place in the world. And until somebody with more juice than me puts this stinker behind bars, I plan on doing my shift and keeping a low profile. I'd suggest you do the same."

"Sorry, no can do."

Harris shook his head in disgust and finally started the engine. "I don't know what that lady means to you, but after what I saw, I've got a pretty good idea. And if you don't start thinking with the brain in your head instead of the one in your pants, you're gonna be knee-deep in trouble."

Rafe supposed he had this coming, but it wasn't like that at all. He was just doing his job.

"Doesn't matter how many times you say it, Phil, I'm not going to change my mind. I don't see any harm in having a nice, civil talk with the man."

Harris huffed and put the cruiser in motion. "It's been a pleasure knowing you, hotshot. Say hello to St. Peter for me."

BACK AT THE STATION HOUSE, Rafe typed up an incident report on the shooting at the garage and dropped it off on Kate's desk. It had taken considerable effort to concentrate on the task, his mind continuously drifting back to Lisa.

Had Phil been right?

Was he thinking with his libido?

The scene in Lisa's living room kept replaying through his mind. Seeing her on that sofa with a sleeping child in her arms. Thinking how time had a way of expanding and contracting. How three years seemed like an eternity—and *had* been when you considered the changes they'd both been through. Yet as he had pulled her into that hug, it felt as if no more than a handful of minutes had passed since he'd last held her.

The feel of her body pressed against his had been so familiar, so comforting—so electric—that he'd had a hard time letting her go.

He thought about the dream he'd had. The one that continued to haunt him. Lisa holding him by the hand, urgently pulling him along a tree-lined trail toward a house near the water.

"Where are we going?" he had asked.

"I want to show you something. Something wonderful. Something glorious."

She continued to pull him along.

"What?" he said. "What is it?"

She threw her head back, the air around

them coming alive with the music of her laughter, a high, sweet trill that had always filled him with joy. "It's a secret, silly. But you'll find out soon enough."

Before they reached that house, however, the house that held the secret, the sound of his alarm had jarred him awake. He had opened his eyes feeling cheated, the remnants of the dream swirling though his head, leaving him with a vague, undefined yearning in the middle of his chest.

In the middle of his heart.

It had been an effort to shake it off and go to work, but he'd done his best, never suspecting that he was about to walk right into that dream. To feel Lisa's touch again, after accepting long ago that she was gone for good.

Was he some kind of psychic?

Was it fate that had brought them together again?

Rafe didn't know or much care. It had been a shock, and a delight, and maybe Phil *was* right. Maybe he was letting his emotions, his desire, override his reason. But he had been trained to protect and serve, and who better to protect than someone he knew? Someone he had loved?

Oliver Sloan was a bad man—worse yet, a

bad man with connections—but if Rafe didn't confront him about Lisa, who would?

Rafe had seen Sloan's type time and again, and he knew full well that unless some-one called him on his behavior, it wouldn't change. Unless Sloan was told, in no uncer-tain terms, to leave Lisa alone, he would be back, and the violence would escalate.

It always did.

So when Rafe finished his report and dropped it on Kate's desk, he didn't bother to shower, didn't bother to change out of his uniform. He ran a quick address check, then went straight to the department garage and signed out a new patrol car.

Then he headed across town to talk to Oli-ver Sloan.

Chapter Seven

Sloan despised himself sometimes.

It didn't happen often, and it was never because of the things he'd done—and he had done quite a few sketchy things in his life.

No, this occasional self-loathing came down to one thing. How he felt. About Lisa, in particular.

His entire life, Sloan had never had trouble getting women. He was, after all, a good-looking guy—something he'd been well aware of since his second birthday.

His mother used to dote on him, call him her little movie star. The girls in middle and high school used to stare at him as he walked the halls, hoping he'd grace them with a glance of his piercing blue eyes. And if you were to put him in a lineup with Brad Pitt and George Clooney, well, let's just say those two cretins would have to fight for attention.

This wasn't ego at work. Sloan merely

saw what he saw when he looked in the mirror, and knew what he knew. And when he snapped his fingers, the women came running as if they hadn't had a meal in a week and were just dying to get a taste of Oliver Sloan.

But that Lisa, she was different.

No amount of good looks and charm could crack its way through that cement wall she'd built around her, and that aggravated Sloan no end. Yet she had gotten so deep under his skin that he felt an itch every time he was around her. A desire so strong that he lost control. Almost felt powerless in her presence.

And Sloan didn't like feeling powerless.

Sloan despised feeling powerless.

As a consequence, at those moments—as rare as they were—he despised himself.

HE HAD WANTED HER the moment he met her, and could still remember the day with great clarity.

He had taken a field trip to the Chicago branch of his real estate firm, and the moment he walked in the door, he saw her, sitting there behind the reception desk. A fresh-faced twenty-three-year-old with a look of innocence that could only be measured in terms of what it did to his body.

Sloan had seen his share of beautiful women in his time, but the sight of Lisa had nearly stopped his heart—a reaction no woman had ever before had on him.

First, there was that face. Like an exquisitely lit photograph of feminine perfection, with flawless white skin, cobalt-blue eyes, and a pouty mouth that was made to do naughty things to naughty boys.

Then there was the body. He couldn't see much behind the reception desk, but what he saw sent a rush of adrenaline coursing through his veins, and he knew he had to have her.

She smiled as he stepped off the elevator, and said, "May I help you?"

Apparently, she hadn't gotten the memo that he'd be visiting today.

"I'm Oliver Sloan," he said, thinking she must be new if she didn't already know that. "I'm here to see Gary Orbach."

She got to her feet then and held out a hand to shake. "Mr. Sloan, I'm Lisa Tobin, and I want thank you for giving me a chance here. This job couldn't have come at a better time."

Sloan didn't do the hiring or firing—that

was beneath him—but he was all too happy to take credit for hiring her. To his surprise, however, now that she was standing up, he could see a slight bulge in the front of her dress.

Was she pregnant?

Not that this killed the effect. In fact, in some odd way it made her even more attractive to him. Maybe because it meant she wasn't a stranger to the kind of carnal activities he was imagining at that very moment.

To his further surprise, he found himself checking her hand for a wedding ring.

There wasn't one.

So did this mean she was one of those unconventional brides who had decided to forgo wearing one in some lame attempt to show her independence? Or was she simply not married at all? And if she wasn't married, was there a boyfriend in the picture? A biological father?

The fact that he even cared was a bit disconcerting. He had never hesitated to hit on a married woman. He was, after all, Oliver Sloan, and nine times out of ten such advances were successful. In fact, *eight* times out of ten even the husband knew what was going on and had the good sense to keep his mouth shut and stay out of the way.

But for some unknown reason, Sloan wanted this one—this Lisa Tobin—this specimen of perfection with the alluring pregnancy bump—to be unattached.

Because he knew the moment he saw her that he had to have her all to himself.

From now until forever.

THEIR COURTSHIP had been short, but fraught with frustration. For Sloan at least.

He quickly discovered that Lisa wasn't like other women. Was not impressed by his looks and his money and his standing in the community. And this, Lord help him, made her even more attractive to him.

It wasn't until long after their separation that he realized that it must have been a ploy. She had manipulated him into wanting her. Wanting her to the point where he broke his cardinal rule and got down on one knee and asked her to marry him.

They had been dating several weeks by then. Dates that had started out tentative and full of hesitation on her part. She had told him that she didn't ever want him to feel that she was taking advantage of him because of the baby. And he had believed her. For no other reason than he was madly, head-over-heels in love with her—an emotional malady that he had always scoffed at.

The powerlessness he felt when he was around her niggled at him, worried him. Made him wonder if he was losing his edge. He remained on his best behavior around her because he didn't want to upset her, take the chance of losing her.

In those first weeks he had even taken a hiatus on bedding other women. And when he finally got *Lisa* into bed, it was the most sublime experience he'd ever been part of. He didn't know where or how she had learned to do what she did, but he didn't care as long as it was with him.

And when she said "yes" to marriage, it was the happiest day of his life.

It wasn't until the baby was born, five months later, that things began to go sour. After Chloe came into the world, Lisa became less attentive and a lot less interested in taking him to bed.

At first he blamed it on postpartum depression, but he quickly grew impatient with her. A man should only have to put up with so much.

And her obsession with Chloe was relentless. Didn't she realize she had a husband to tend to? Didn't she understand that it was only his generosity that had allowed her to spend so much time with the child?

He had offered to get Chloe a nanny, so that Lisa would be free of the responsibilities of raising the kid, but Lisa had balked at the idea. Said she was only interested in raising Chloe herself, and wished that Sloan would be more attentive to the little girl he had promised to raise.

He didn't remember making such a promise, but he supposed somewhere in the haze of bedding Lisa and asking her to marry him, he must have made noises in that direction. But surely she had to understand that such promises were never meant to be kept. He was all too happy to support the kid, but he didn't have time to be developing a relationship with her, any more than his father had had time for him.

This seemed to be a sticking point with Lisa, however, and he soon realized that she didn't love him the way she once had. That the freshness of spirit that was there in the beginning of their relationship had all but disappeared.

And this made him need her even more. He found himself constantly consumed by thoughts of her, wondering what he could to do to regain what they'd lost. He found himself taking out his frustration on the other women he bedded. Had even broken the jaw of one of them when she'd had the audacity to ask if Lisa cared that he had strayed.

And when Lisa found out about it and confronted him, he had been open and honest with her in hopes that she would realize what she was doing to him.

Instead, she had gotten crafty. She'd begun sneaking around in his personal files and had told him that if he didn't grant her a divorce, he would pay the consequences.

It was only then that Sloan realized he had been used. That she had only pretended not to care about his money. That there was undoubtedly another man out there telling her what to do. How to manipulate Sloan.

Yet, oddly enough, none of that mattered.

He still wanted her, more than ever. The year of separation had been sheer torture for him and he couldn't convince himself that it was over.

No matter what it took, he would get her back. And this time, it would be on *his* terms, not hers. He was, after all, the man in this relationship and it was time he made her realize that.

This morning may have backfired with that nosy maid of hers brandishing a shotgun, but there would be other days. Other mornings.

And sooner or later, Sloan would have what rightfully belonged to him.

Chapter Eight

It wasn't a surprise that Sloan didn't live in a house. No, a guy like him only *owned* houses. Living in one would be far too conventional for him. He was a mover and a shaker who considered himself to be movie-star cool. So what better way to prove it than to live in a hotel suite?

But not just *any* hotel. Sloan lived in one of the most luxurious establishments in St. Louis. The one with a five-room penthouse suite priced at four grand a night, with a name fit for a king.

The Palace.

Rafe had only been here on a couple previous occasions. Callouts in the middle of the night when some of the guests had gotten unruly. The hotel staff usually handled such matters in-house, with their private security squad, but sometimes things got out of hand

and the Sheriff's department was called in to clean up.

Rafe had always been a meat-and-potatoes kind of guy. Not one for fancy trappings and over-the-top displays of wealth and power. So when he stepped into the Palace lobby, he took in its stark, postmodern decor with a jaundiced eye, thinking about how much meat and potatoes you could buy just by auctioning off its contents.

You could probably feed a small, developing country.

Rafe had no problem with wealth—people deserved to be rewarded for their hard work—but such displays got him wondering about the world's priorities. And it didn't surprise him that Oliver Sloan would choose a place like this to live.

What better cover for his thuggery?

But then Sloan was a new kind of thug. One who used money and power and influence rather than guns—unless, of course, they were absolutely necessary. He wore the finest clothing, dined at the most popular restaurants, smiled for photographs with the elite of St. Louis, pretending to be an upstanding citizen, as he worked his shady deals in back rooms and private offices.

Rafe knew that if he tried to go through channels to see Sloan, if he went to the front desk and sent up a message, he would be turned away. And if he pressed it, if he insisted on being seen, then Sloan's cronies would be alerted, management and security staff would appear out of nowhere and Rafe's boss would be dragged out of bed by a call from someone on high asking how some insignificant sheriff's deputy had the audacity to show up on Sloan's doorstep at six o'clock in the morning.

That was a scene Rafe would just as soon avoid. So the moment he walked into the hotel, he turned to the bellman on duty and gestured abruptly.

"Follow me," he said.

The bellman's eyes widened slightly at the sight of Rafe's uniform, but he didn't balk, didn't resist. Instead, he nodded politely and came around from his desk and followed Rafe straight to the bank of elevators on the far side of the lobby.

Rafe pushed the button, waited for the doors to open, then gestured the bellman inside. "After you."

As they turned to face the closing doors, Rafe said, "Take me to the penthouse."

He had known that getting there would require special access and only a bellman or the hotel manager would have the key.

But now the bellman balked. He just stood there without moving.

So did the elevator.

"Well?" Rafe said.

"I, uh, I'm not supposed to let anyone up there."

Rafe had been expecting this.

"I feel your pain, but you're just going to have to steel yourself and make an exception."

"But we have strict orders from Mr. Sloan to—"

"You see this uniform?" Rafe said.

"Uh…yeah."

"You think I'm wearing it just for fun?"

"Uh…no."

"I'm a deputy with the St. Louis Sheriff's Department, and I don't care what Mr. Sloan ordered you to do. When I tell you to take me to the penthouse, you'd better take me to the penthouse or you'll find yourself facing a possible obstruction of justice charge. Do you want that?"

The bellman swallowed, said nothing. He just reached into his pocket, took out a key card and slipped it into a slot on the elevator panel, punching a button with his index finger.

The elevator glided into motion. Rafe put his trust in the numbers that lit up the panel above the doors to be sure they were actually moving.

When they reached the penthouse, a faint bell chimed and the doors slid open again. Beyond them was a long, richly appointed hallway, bathed in white. There was another set of doors at the far end, two dark-suited guards keeping watch in front of them.

Rafe thanked the bellman and started down the hall, wondering if he should have brought a pair of hiking shoes for the trek. He once again marveled that Lisa had been married—if only briefly—to a guy this far out of touch with reality, and decided he'd definitely have to get that "long story" on record.

Not that she owed him any explanations. But he was curious, and hoped she'd be willing to share.

He was about halfway down the hall when one of Sloan's guards said, "Excuse me, deputy, but we weren't informed of your arrival. Do you have an appointment?"

"It's six o'clock in the morning," Rafe said.

"Who makes an appointment at six o'clock in the morning?"

"Then I can only assume you got off on the wrong floor." The guy may have looked classy and all in his suit, but the tenor and tone of his voice betrayed him as just another thug.

"You can assume all you want," Rafe told him. "But I'm here to see Mr. Sloan about his early-morning activities. So wake him up if you have to."

The thug smiled as Rafe came to a stop in front of him. "I'm getting the impression you don't know how this works."

"You *should* be getting the impression that I don't care. Tell Sloan I'm here."

"You aren't too smart, are you?" the other guard said.

"Smart enough to make it through college, for what it's worth. What year did *you* drop out?"

"Hey, Frank," the first one said, apparently addressing his partner. "We got ourselves a comedian."

"I think you're right," Frank said.

"Remember that funny guy out in Vegas? The one who kept cracking jokes about your crew cut?"

"The guy who kept calling me G.I. Joe? Yeah, I remember."

"Wasn't he a fed or something?"

"Narcotics detective," Frank said. "And come to think of it, he tried to get in to see Mr. Sloan without an appointment, too."

"You ever find out what happened to him?"

Frank shrugged. "Last I heard, the brace was off, but he was still in physical therapy."

Now they both turned their gazes on Rafe, their faces abruptly hardening, their eyes full of quiet menace. These were two men who took their jobs very seriously and answered only to one master.

And it wasn't Rafe.

He said, "Come on, guys, why the hostility? All you have to do is open that door and step aside and let me talk to your boss. I'll even apologize for the 'dropout' crack."

Rafe knew he was wasting his breath, but he was simply waiting for one of them to make the inevitable move. They were done talking and ready to introduce Rafe to their fists, and he was trying to decide which one would take the lead.

As is turned out, they moved simultaneously, like a well-choreographed dance duo, one reaching for Rafe's jacket as the other took a swing.

But Rafe hadn't spent the past few years just lifting weights. A month after joining the department, he had signed up for a self-defense class, led by a guy who specialized in Krav Maga. He had gotten so good at it that he now led the class himself, every Tuesday and Thursday night.

It took four precise moves to put Frank out of commission and pin his partner to the floor, all without breaking much of a sweat.

Now Frank was unconscious and the other one was looking up at Rafe with eyes that were no longer filled with menace, but with the kind of desperation that only a man fearing for his life can produce.

But Rafe wasn't a sadist. He gave the guy a polite warning, then released him and stepped toward the hotel suite doors.

"Don't worry," he said, "I'll announce myself."

RAFE HAD BEEN EXPECTING more thugs inside the suite, but was pleasantly surprised when no one came rushing forward.

The suite, which was triple the size of his apartment, looked like something out of a lifestyle magazine, with a flawless white carpet and a handcrafted sofa and chairs that were clearly more expensive than the pieces he sat on at home.

Off to his right was a full kitchen featuring a state-of-the-art espresso bar. Being a Franco, Rafe was a sucker for a good shot, so it immediately caught his attention.

To the left were two open doorways that he assumed led to bedrooms. And judging by the sounds emanating from one of them, and the long trail of male and female clothing leading directly to it, his assessment was accurate.

He didn't doubt that it was Sloan in there. The guy had worked up an appetite with Lisa and was now quenching it with someone who would give him what Lisa hadn't been willing to. They were making quite a racket, those two, so Rafe went to the espresso bar, made himself a shot, then settled in on the sofa to wait for them to finish up.

Chapter Nine

"Who the hell are *you?*" Sloan barked.

He stood naked in the bedroom doorway, his muscular body bathed in sweat, a scowl on his face as he stared at Rafe with eyes full of rage. He was about thirty-five, with short dark hair, and held a pair of boxer shorts in his right hand—which he had scooped up from the floor before realizing Rafe was there.

Lisa had said he was drunk when he came to her house, and the effects of the alcohol—and whatever else he was ingesting—didn't seem to have worn off.

Rafe set the espresso cup on the coffee table and got to his feet, nodding to the scattered clothes. "You want to get dressed, Mr. Sloan? I can wait."

But Sloan obviously wasn't embarrassed by his nakedness. He made no move to cover himself. "How did you get in here?"

"Your guards let me in."

"What?"

"I was as surprised as you are," Rafe said. "I guess my people skills are a lot better than I thought they were."

Sloan finally started pulling the boxers on. "Do you have a warrant?"

"For what? I'm not here to search the premises. I just want to talk."

Sloan scooped up a pair of dark slacks. "Then make an appointment. I want you out of here. Now."

Rafe smiled. "You know, it's funny. I'm pretty sure that's what Lisa Tobin wanted when you paid her a visit early this morning. Yet it took a shotgun to get you to leave."

"Lisa?" Sloan said incredulously. "You're here because of Lisa?"

"You assaulted her, Mr. Sloan. Physically."

Sloan scowled again. "I didn't do any such thing." He started jabbing his legs into the pants, angrily punctuating his words. "My ex-wife is a pathological liar. And you're an idiot if you believe a word she says."

"Oh? What about the housekeeper? Beatrice. Was she lying, too?"

Sloan scoffed. "Do you know I hired that ungrateful witch? She's as nutty as Lisa is."

"Maybe so, but Ms. Tobin seemed very upset, and I have a hard time believing she was lying about what happened."

"Lisa Tobin is very good at manipulating men into thinking she's some kind of victim. But what she really does is use them, then discard them when they're no longer useful to her."

"Or maybe she just doesn't like being cheated on," Rafe said. "By men who brutalize their mistresses."

Sloan was in the middle of buttoning his shirt now, but stopped abruptly and looked at Rafe. "You're gonna want to watch your step, deputy."

"Or what?"

Sloan moved toward him and Rafe instinctively dropped his hand to his Glock.

"How old are you?" he said. "Twenty-five, twenty-six? You're barely out of diapers and you think you know it all, don't you? Think because you wear that fancy uniform and that star on your chest that you can barge into a man's home and make accusations about his character."

"You can't be that clueless about your reputation," Rafe said.

"My reputation? I'm a businessman."

"Is that what they're calling it these days?"

Sloan raised his right hand and held his thumb and forefinger in a pinch, leaving less than a quarter-inch of space between them. "You're that close to getting your butt kicked, hotshot."

"By whom? Frank and his girlfriend in the hall? They've already tried and it didn't work out so well."

Sloan studied him a moment. "I've got to admit you've got brass in your pants, deputy. But I can't help wondering why you're really here."

"Just to tell you to back off. Leave Lisa alone."

Sloan smiled. "So it's Lisa now, is it? Did she bat those baby blues at you and get you all aquiver inside?" He paused. "Or maybe it's more than that. Maybe she gave you a little taste of the goods and you came up here to play knight in shining armor."

"You really like to hear yourself talk, don't you?"

Sloan shrugged. "I can think of worse ways to spend the day."

"Well, maybe you should listen for a minute. If you think you can walk into a house, a house with your own child in it, and—"

"My own child?" Sloan chuckled. "You don't know *anything,* do you?"

"I know it's my job to butt heads with jerks like you," Rafe said. "And if you think you can terrorize women without consequences, keep pushing, buddy. I'm all too happy to push back."

Sloan stared at him and Rafe returned the stare, the tension between them palpable. Volatile. Part of Rafe hoped that Sloan would make a move. Give him a reason to bring out the cuffs.

But Sloan was no dummy. He suddenly relaxed. Finished buttoning his shirt. "As I said, deputy, I didn't go anywhere near that house this morning. I've been in this suite since ten o'clock last night, and I've got half a dozen witnesses who'll vouch for me. Including the little gal you just heard moaning and groaning." He grinned. "And she wasn't faking it."

"You're pathetic, you know that?"

"Be that as it may," Sloan said, "I live in a world you can only dream about, and that gives me certain privileges. You made a big mistake coming here, hotshot. I figure by this time tomorrow morning you'll be looking for a way to pay your rent, and you're usefulness to my ex-wife will have come to an abrupt, unceremonious end."

"Or I could just beat the crap out of you and claim self-defense. Arrest you for attempted assault on a sheriff's deputy."

Sloan smiled again. "Ah, but you wouldn't do that, would you? I know your kind. You're Deputy Dudley Do-Right, who helps damsels in distress and believes in the letter of the law." He tucked his shirt in and turned, heading toward the doorway he had emerged from. When he reached it, he turned back, still smiling. "I think you can find your way out, deputy. And when you go, be sure to tell Frank and Bobby that their services are no longer—"

"Hey, baby, what's the holdup?" A naked woman with tousled blond hair appeared in the doorway behind him. "Do you want another toot or not?"

She was carrying a baggie full of white powder, her pinky extended toward him, the hollow of her long, scarlet-colored fingernail loaded with the stuff.

Rafe couldn't believe his good fortune. Fate once again stepping in when he least expected it, giving him an excuse to draw his weapon and point it at Sloan and the woman.

"Down!" he shouted. "On your knees! Now!"

The woman yelped in surprise, dropping the baggie as Sloan gave her a murderous look, then threw his hands in the air and sank to the carpet.

"Don't shoot, don't shoot!" she cried, quickly mimicking Sloan.

As she dropped to her knees, Rafe reached for the radio still clipped to his shoulder and flicked it on. "Dispatch, I've got a 190 in progress and I need backup."

He gave them the address, then gestured to the clothes that remained on the floor and told Sloan's companion to put them on.

Sloan looked up at him, fire in his eyes. "Better start getting that resume in order, hotshot. And I sure hope you've got experience cleaning toilets, because when I'm done with you, that's about the only job you'll be able to get."

"Stop," Rafe said. "You're scaring me."

But as he looked into Sloan's eyes, he could see that this was far from over.

Chapter Ten

Lisa wasn't able to go back to sleep that morning.

After Rafe and his partner left, Beatrice had scooped up Chloe from the sofa and carried her upstairs, announcing that she was headed back to bed.

"I bought some eggs if you want breakfast," she said. "And the coffeemaker's set on automatic."

Lisa knew Bea wasn't happy with her. Her words had come out in a clipped monotone that telegraphed her displeasure. Bea felt that failing to press charges against Oliver was a mistake. That he had gotten away with too much in his life because people were afraid of him.

And maybe she was right. Maybe Lisa *should* have pressed charges. But, until tonight, Oliver had never laid a finger on her and she knew that much of what had happened here had been fueled by the drugs and alcohol.

There was actually a time when Oliver had been sweet to her. Kind. And despite that sense of menace she felt around him now, despite the episode with that other woman—the one that had led to their divorce—Lisa had a hard time equating the man she had married with the picture Rafe and his partner had painted.

So when it came time to pull the trigger—to use one of Oliver's favorite phrases—she couldn't bring herself to do it. A mistake, perhaps, but it was *her* mistake and she would own it, just as she owned all the others she'd made.

Her inability to sleep, however, had nothing to do with Oliver. The significance of what had happened with him in this room paled in comparison to what had followed.

Lisa had long ago given up on the thought of ever seeing Rafe Franco again, had convinced herself that he no longer mattered to her. She had assumed that he had stayed in California and was spending his weekends on the shores of Malibu or Zuma Beach or one of the other sun-and-fun hot spots they'd seen on television.

But suddenly here he was, the man she had loved so fervently. The first—and only—real love she had ever known. He was no longer a confused, idealistic college student, but a grounded sheriff's deputy who commanded a room when he entered it.

The transformation Rafe had undergone was startling to Lisa, but in a good way. Three years ago, when they parted ways, she had been convinced that he was too young and restless to commit to her. That trying to tie him down would be a mistake, even if she loved him more than anyone she'd ever known.

It was *because* of that love that she had let him go. Had even pretended that she, too, was restless. That she, *too,* wanted to explore the possibilities of life. They had talked about going their separate ways many times in that last year of college, and she knew that Rafe needed time to find himself.

So she had given it to him, even after she found out she was pregnant.

When the doctor sprang the news, Lisa's first instinct had been to try to contact Rafe. To tell him he was about to be a father. Rafe was just the type of guy to drop everything, to put his life on hold and do the right thing. To marry her and help her raise their child.

But the last thing she wanted was a marriage based on obligation. Her parents had married because of *her,* and they had been miserable for as long as she could remember.

So she had never picked up that phone, had never sent him that email. Had convinced herself that *this* was the right thing to do. To grant Rafe his freedom.

But seeing him walk into her living room had changed everything. Seeing him look down at Chloe and smile, hearing him tell her how beautiful Chloe was, had made her realize that the choice she'd made might very well have been the wrong one. That it wasn't fair to Rafe.

Or to Chloe.

But after more than three years, how could she possibly break the news to him? She couldn't simply blurt out, "Oh, by the way, Chloe is yours."

She had to find the right moment.

The perfect moment.

But when, she wondered, would that be?

"So TELL ME ABOUT that hunk of a deputy," Bea said.

She had awakened an hour later in a much

better mood. Had poured herself a cup of coffee and sat at the kitchen table, where Lisa was staring forlornly at a bowl of fruit and yogurt.

"He's just a guy I knew in college," Lisa said, trying to downplay the relationship. Bea had no idea that Chloe was that "hunk" of a deputy's baby. Nobody did.

Bea grinned. "*Knew?* As in the biblical sense?"

It was just like the woman to get straight to the point. Lisa didn't bother to respond, but she felt her face grow warm and Bea's grin widened.

"Atta girl, Leese. Believe me, if I were forty years younger, that's one piece of man-candy I wouldn't mind taking a tumble with."

"That was a long time ago," Lisa said.

"Oh, who cares. At least you've got the memory. And I'll bet he was pretty memorable, too."

Lisa felt a smile coming on and tried but failed to stifle it. "I won't deny we were pretty good together."

"Well," Bea said, "he seemed happy to see you, and I noticed he didn't have a ring on his finger."

Lisa had to admit that she'd noticed, too.

And the moment she did, she had experienced an inexplicable feeling of relief, and maybe a little hope. But then her mother—who was a virulently unhappy woman—had always said that hope was for dreamers.

Besides, Lisa wasn't interested in trapping Rafe now any more than she had been after college.

"I'm not looking to get married again," she said to Bea. "Not after this last disaster."

"Well, I can't blame you for that. But don't let one nasty apple spoil the entire barrel for you. Besides, I've got a feeling Deputy Studly will keep to his promise and do a little damage repair on your behalf."

"And what if it doesn't stick?" Lisa asked.

"Then you do what you should've done in the first place and file charges against that no-good ex of yours."

"And what if that doesn't stick, either?"

"Then I guess Mr. Oliver Sloan'll find out just how good of a shot I really am…"

Chapter Eleven

"I don't think you realize just how danger-
ously close you are to getting yourself fired."

Harold Pine was captain of the Patrol Division, a thirty-year veteran who hadn't been in
the field in more than half that time.

He sat behind his desk, his tailored uniform
masking his considerable bulk. There was
little he could do, however, about his slightly
misshapen dome, which he regularly shaved
bald in an attempt to look slick—an attempt
that failed on many different levels.

Rafe shifted in the chair in front of Pine's
desk. "I was just doing my job," he said.
Which wasn't strictly true, since Lisa hadn't
filed a complaint against Sloan.

"Your job?" Pine barked. "Your job is to
follow protocol. Nothing more, nothing less."

After calling for backup at Sloan's hotel
suite, Rafe had done a quick sweep of the
rooms and found another cache of cocaine,

along with several tabs of what looked like ecstasy. But now Sloan's girlfriend was claiming the drugs were hers, and his attorney was screaming illegal search and seizure, charging that Rafe had been in the hotel suite not on police business, but as a private citizen.

In other words, he had been trespassing and had no probable cause for the search. And to Rafe's surprise, not only had the judge at the morning arraignment agreed with Sloan's attorney, but so did Pine.

"No, what you did was screw up, Franco. I talked to Deputy Harris and I know exactly what happened. You aren't the first cop to get his weenie in a knot over a woman, but you chose the wrong ex-husband to go after."

"Why?" Rafe said. "Everyone in the department knows Sloan is dirty. This was our chance to put him away."

"There's just one small problem with that."

"Which is?"

Pine smiled patiently, then got to his feet. "There are some people who want to talk to you."

He gestured and Rafe stood up, following him out the door. They moved down a long corridor to a conference room, Rafe wondering what was going on until Pine threw open the door to reveal who was inside.

The were four people seated at the conference table, two of whom Rafe had seen earlier that morning: his sister Kate and her partner, Charlie Eberhart. Sitting beside them was Kate's boss, Captain Weeks, and at the head of the table was none other than the County Undersheriff himself—the man Kate was rumored to be dating—Daniel Macon.

As the door closed behind Rafe, Macon gestured. "Have a seat, deputy."

Rafe did as he was told. He glanced at Kate, but her face was a mask. He had no earthly idea what this was all about, but figured he would soon find out.

And he knew it couldn't be good.

Once Rafe was settled in his seat, Macon said, "I'm sure you're aware, Deputy Franco, that Oliver Sloan has long been a target of this department."

Rafe nodded. "I know he's been a thorn in our side for quite some time."

"And I'm sure," Macon continued, "that you thought arresting Sloan on a petty drug charge was a way to put him behind bars where he belongs."

"I didn't go there to arrest him," Rafe said.

"Just talk to him. I saw the drugs, and did my duty."

"Be that as it may," Kate said, "you also jeopardized a nine-month-long investigation."

Surprised, Rafe swiveled his head toward her. "Investigation?"

"The woman you arrested along with Sloan was an undercover operative for this department. She's been one of my confidential informants for years."

"That's right, genius," Eberhart told him. "You just cowboyed your way into an ongoing investigation and nearly blew the whole thing."

Rafe was speechless. What was there to say? No words he uttered would change what had happened.

But how could he be blamed for this? He may have gone to Sloan's hotel suite for personal reasons, but the bust he'd made had been righteous. By the book.

Was he about to be hung out to dry for doing his duty?

"Fortunately," Macon said, "the judge saw fit to drop the charges against him. A judge we think could very well be in Oliver Sloan's pocket. Only this time it worked to our advantage."

Kate leaned forward. "But do you see the stakes we're dealing with here? This isn't just about Oliver Sloan. It's about the network he's built and all the people who are beholden to him."

"Including his ex-wife," Eberhart said.

Rafe stiffened, felt the hairs on the back of his neck rise. Were they suggesting that Lisa was part of Sloan's criminal organization?

That was ridiculous.

First, Rafe knew she'd never get involved in any illegal activities—not now, not ever. Three and a half years couldn't have changed her *that* much. And second, her reaction to the truth about her ex-husband's activities had been genuine. Even if she had suspected that Sloan was up to no good, it was obvious that such suspicions had been vague and ill-formed, and nothing to do with organized crime.

"We understand his ex is an old girlfriend of yours," Macon said.

Rafe nodded. "We dated in college."

"And where was that?"

"University of Illinois."

"He pretty much kept her under wraps, too," Kate said with a smile. "Only brought her out here once during all that time and I never even got a chance to meet her. I guess he didn't want to expose her to the fighting Francos."

Rafe chafed. "Why does any of this matter?"

Kate's boss, Captain Weeks, spoke up. "Because," he said, "we think this unexpected reunion is extraordinarily fortunate. A turn of events that could be used to our advantage."

Rafe felt his gut tighten. "What do you mean?"

"It's simple," Macon told him. "We want you to turn her. We want you to nurture the relationship and convince her to be our confidential informant."

Rafe couldn't quite believe what he was hearing.

"So let me get this straight," he said. "You want me to betray a friendship in order to get at Sloan?"

"Not betray," Kate said. "Merely talk her into helping us."

"What about the blonde? Your CI?"

"Unfortunately, I've already heard from her. Even though she claimed the drugs, she says that Sloan blames her for the bust and told her to get lost. She thinks it'll be a long time before she can get him to trust her again."

Rafe considered this for a moment. He had no intention of agreeing to their demand, but he was curious what they figured they could get out of it.

"And if I were to turn Lisa," he said, "what exactly would you expect her to do?"

Macon spread his hands out. "Judging by that domestic call, it's obvious that Sloan still harbors some feelings for his ex-wife and his child. We'd want her to encourage his affection and try to—"

Rafe abruptly stood up. "You're out of your mind if you think I'd do that to her."

"We aren't really asking, Deputy Franco. Your future with the department could well depend on your decision."

Rafe shot Kate a look, surprised that she would be part of this.

She gave him a brief, apologetic shrug, as if to say *This wasn't my call,* then quickly looked down and studied the tabletop.

"Well, Deputy Franco? You do value your future here, don't you?"

"Not if it means taking advantage of someone I care about. I took this job to help people, not manipulate them. That's the kind of thing Sloan would do."

"Law enforcement can sometimes be dirty business," Captain Weeks said. "And we have to fight fire with fire."

Rafe shook his head. "Not with me, you won't."

Then he turned and walked out the door.

KATE CAUGHT UP TO HIM in the hallway. "Rafe, wait."

He stopped, turned, his body stiff with fury. It was bad enough they were asking him to betray Lisa, but he couldn't quite fathom why his own sister would be part of it.

"I know this stinks," she said. "And I'm sorry you got caught in the middle of it. But the truth is, you kind of put yourself there."

"I busted a man for possession of drugs. Last I heard, that was considered a good thing."

"You have to understand the stakes here, Rafe. We've been after this jerk for nearly a year now and so far we've got nothing."

Rafe's eyebrows went up. "Not even from your CI?"

Kate shook her head. "Sloan's been very careful to keep his business to himself. My

CI has even tried searching his computer, but couldn't find anything incriminating."

"Then maybe you're wasting your time. Maybe you should've been happy with the drug bust."

Kate snorted. "Oh, yeah," she said. "And if we got lucky, if Sloan was actually convicted, he'd get maybe five years. Less for a first offense. In the meantime, his network stays intact and he gets out of prison even richer and more powerful than he is now."

Rafe stared at her. "I'm not going to try to turn Lisa, Kate."

"And I'm not asking you to, Rafe. Do you think I wanted this? I know how much she meant to you back in college, even if you did keep your love life under wraps."

"Then why are we even doing this?"

"For two reasons," Kate said. "First, Oliver Sloan is a very bad man. You know those bodies you found this morning? We think he may be behind that."

Rafe had figured the hits were mob-related. So it made sense that Sloan was somehow involved.

But that didn't change anything.

"The second?" he asked her.

Kate's eyes softened. "I'm worried about

you, little brother. I know it took you a long time and a lot of soul searching before you decided to join the family business. And I'd hate to see this decision destroy it for you before you've really had a chance to prove yourself."

"If proving myself means what you people seem to think it means, then maybe I'm not cut out for the family business."

"Just think it over," she said. "Who knows? This could even mean that bump up to Homicide you want so badly. Take a day or two. I'll stall the others."

"You can stall them all you want," Rafe told her. "I'm not going to change my mind."

"Believe me, I know how stubborn you can be. And I don't want you to do anything that would compromise your beliefs. But take the time anyway, okay?"

"Whatever you say, sis."

Rafe gave her a look, then turned and walked away.

Chapter Twelve

Sloan wanted Rafe Franco's head.

All he could think about as he sat in that disgusting, foul-smelling jail cell was how miserable Deputy Do-Right was about to be.

This guy Franco thought he had it all figured out. Thought he could come into Sloan's hotel room, terrorize his woman, slap cuffs on his wrists and actually get away with it.

Hadn't he gotten the memo?

Nobody messed with Oliver Sloan.

Nobody.

Rafe Franco was about to be educated. You don't go after a man like Sloan and come out smelling like roses. Instead, you'd be smelling like what those roses are *planted* in, and the stench won't be going away anytime soon.

In fact, you'd be very lucky if *you* weren't planted along with them.

Five hours, Sloan thought. Five hours he sat fuming in that cell, hours he'd never be able to get back. Hours he could've spent boffing that little blond Gloria—if she hadn't been stupid enough to come trotting out of his bedroom buck naked with a bag of coke in hand.

Stupid, stupid, stupid.

Then there were Frank and Bobby. Those two were supposed to *prevent* guys like Franco from getting into the hotel suite.

And what had they done?

Folded like a couple of lawn chairs.

When Franco booked him, the first thing Sloan did was demand his phone call. He pulled his lawyer out of bed and put her to work. Sloan had three things he wanted taken care of by the time they got to court that morning.

First, a nice little payoff arranged for the judge who was scheduled to do the arraignment. Fortunately, it turned out they already had a standing financial agreement with the guy, so the problem was easily taken care of.

Second was to get him a decent suit to wear to court. The clothes he'd managed to put on before the shouting started and the cuffs came out were wrinkled and soiled—partly with Gloria's cherry-red lipstick. Sloan had a reputation to maintain, and refused to appear in public without a perfectly pressed suit, a crisp shirt and a neatly knotted tie. His old man had always told him that you're more often judged by what you wear than what you do or say, and it was Sloan's experience that those words were absolutely true.

The third item on his lawyer's agenda was to check into this idiot Rafe Franco. Sloan had sensed that Franco hadn't come to the hotel as an officer of the law, and he wanted to know exactly what the nature of his relationship with Lisa might be.

Was he her boyfriend?

Had he been sleeping with her?

If so, how had he escaped Sloan's surveillance? Sloan had been putting teams on Lisa since the day they separated. Not *every* day, mind you, but enough to keep tabs. And he couldn't for the life of him figure how they had managed to miss her playing nighty-night with a six-foot-two-inch hunk of stone.

So finding out what Lisa and Franco had between them was high priority. Sloan would be damned if he'd let some cop steal Lisa's heart. For better or worse, that heart belonged to Sloan and Sloan only, whether she liked it or not. It was bought and paid for, baby. Same as her body.

And *that* was something Sloan was willing to kill for.

"THERE HE IS!"

The shout came from a punk of a reporter who looked all of twenty years old. A snot-nosed little creep who probably thought he was the next Woodward or Bernstein. Except in these days of blogs instead of newspapers, pretty much anyone could make that claim. Didn't mean they had what it took to live up to it.

A crowd of reporters and video cameras waited just outside the prisoner processing room, where Sloan had picked up his wallet and personal effects. The crowd wasn't as big as he had expected, and he was a little disappointed by that. There was no such thing as bad publicity as far as he was concerned, and he planned to spin this disaster in his favor.

As she escorted him outside, however, his attorney—a luscious little number in a tight skirt, named Lola Berletti—told him to keep his mouth shut.

"You can't be serious," he snapped.

"You don't want to give them ammunition," she told him. "They'll cherry-pick whatever you say and use it against you."

Sloan huffed a chuckle. "I didn't get where I am by being shy, baby. How about you keep *your* mouth shut and let *me* worry about the press."

Before she could say anything more, the reporters surrounded them, hounding Sloan all the way to the limo. His bodyguards—Frank and Bobby's replacements—made a path as he smiled for the cameras and ignored the inane questions being hurled at him.

But as his driver opened the limo's rear door and Berletti climbed inside, Sloan stopped and turned, facing the cameras and video cam lenses.

"This is much ado about nothing, folks. Much ado about nothing."

A voice rang out above the others. "Is it true there were drugs found in your hotel suite?"

Sloan smiled. "This is simply a case of an overzealous sheriff's deputy who decided to jump to conclusions and arrest everyone in…"

He paused, and the reporters seized the moment, jumping in with more questions. But Sloan's thoughts had been abruptly interrupted. Just beyond their heads, directly in his line of sight, was Rafe Franco, standing in the doorway of the processing center, giving him the cold eye.

Sloan gave it right back, thinking how much he was going to enjoy crushing this jerk.

He cleared his throat and returned his attention to the reporters. "Any drugs that were found in my hotel," he said, "belonged to the young woman I was entertaining and had nothing to do with me. I wasn't even aware she had them—and the court record reflects that." He gave them another smile. "I guess this is ultimately a lesson in how to choose your friends."

More questions came at him rapid-fire, but he again ignored them, shooting Franco one last look as he climbed into the limo and let his driver close him inside.

Berletti was frowning at him. Her skirt was so tight she had to sit at a kind of sideways angle on the seat. She had unbuttoned a couple of buttons on her blouse, revealing that nice mound of cleavage that Sloan had always admired.

"Glad you decided to take my advice," she said.

"I don't pay you for advice," he told her. "I pay you for results. Did you get that information on Deputy Hotshot?"

"Of course. Did you think I'd fail you, O Mighty One?"

Sloan scowled. "Stow the sarcasm, all right? Just give me the info."

Berletti leaned forward, giving him a better look at the valley between her breasts, and reached into her briefcase, pulling out a small computer tablet. She pressed a button, bringing it to life, then tapped an icon, opening a data file.

Rafe Franco's Sheriff's department ID filled the screen, along with a printed narrative.

"Rafael Thomas Franco," she read. "Twenty-six years old this coming July, graduated with honors from the University of—"

"Now why do I give a flying fruitcake where this guy graduated from college?"

"Because it's pertinent information."

"How so?"

"He attended the University of Illinois at Chicago. Which is where he met Lisa Jean Tobin."

Sloan was surprised. Lisa had never mentioned the guy. Had they been in contact all this time?

"So what are you saying? They were college sweethearts?"

"Well," Berletti told him, "that's a little hard to determine on short notice. But take a look at this photo. It's from the Chicago Maroon."

She touched the screen and showed him a page from what looked like a college newspaper featuring a color photo of an art exhibit at the school. Standing in front of an iron sculpture were a young man and woman holding hands.

Sloan had to squint, but he had no doubts that the woman in the photo was Lisa. He'd recognize that angel face anywhere. And the guy holding her hand looked about thirty pounds of muscle lighter, but it was definitely Deputy Franco.

"That seems pretty conclusive to me," he said.

"Well, it's easy to jump to conclusions, but I'd say it's a safe bet they were intimate." She paused. "And the timing is interesting, as well."

"How so?"

"This photo was taken in the latter half of 2009. If they were intimate before they eventually split, then there's every possibility that…" She paused.

"That what?"

"That Mr. Franco is Chloe's father."

Sloan felt a slow burn coming on. Now that

he knew that Franco might well be the guy who had put that kid in Lisa's belly, he had to wonder if Franco had been behind the scenes from the very beginning. Using Lisa to steal Sloan's heart and get to his money.

It didn't seem that far-fetched.

"I want to hurt this creep," he said to Berletti. "I want to hurt him bad."

Sloan thought about this. He could have the guy whacked and it would be over and done with.

But where was the fun in that?

No, he wanted this clown to suffer first. Maybe spend some time in a stinking jail cell himself. Get Lisa and every one of his friends and coworkers looking at him as a loser, a no-good. Get Lisa thinking that maybe she was better off with a real man, like Sloan.

Then he'd have him killed.

He told Berletti all this, and, true to form, she came up with a plan.

"You know those two Russians we took care of last night?"

"Yeah. What about them?"

"Turns out Deputy Franco was the officer who handled the call."

"So?"

"So what if we play with the evidence a

bit and make his associates at the Sheriff's department wonder if he did more than just answer a call?"

Sloan smiled. "You can arrange that?"

Berletti smiled right back, then leaned forward in her seat and kissed Sloan on the mouth. Her breath was hot and her lips tasted like apples.

She took hold of his hand and placed it on one of those voluptuous mounds. "I can arrange anything you want, darling. All I have to do is mention your name..."

Chapter Thirteen

When the doorbell rang, Lisa called out to Beatrice and told her she'd answer it. Chloe was awake now and wreaking havoc on a coloring book at the coffee table, so Lisa patted her head and crossed to the foyer.

"I'll be right back, hon."

When she opened the door, she was surprised and thrilled to see Rafe standing there. He was still wearing his uniform, but the car in the drive behind him was a red Mustang.

"Is this a bad time?" he asked.

The truth was, she hadn't been able to stop thinking about him. Her mind was a mix of emotions—elation, concern, fear—and she still hadn't figured out how to tell him about Chloe. Part of her just wanted to blurt it out, but another part knew that such a strategy—if you could call it one—was ill-advised.

She had no idea where Rafe's head was

right now, and was terrified by the thought that he might not consider this welcome news.

What exactly was she supposed to say?

Oh, by the way, you see that little girl who looks a lot like a cross between you and Shirley Temple? The one with the blond curls and the blue eyes and the cute little dimples? The one you said was beautiful?

That's your daughter, Rafe.

Your *daughter...*

Sorry I never mentioned her to you.

"Leese? Is this a bad time?"

Lisa pulled herself from her thoughts and smiled at him. "No, of course not. I'm just a little distracted by everything that's happened this morning."

He nodded. "I can't blame you. That's why I'm here."

Lisa eyed him hopefully. "You got Oliver to back off? To promise he won't bother me anymore?"

Rafe's expression said he'd done anything but. He looked crestfallen and maybe just a little angry.

"May I come in?"

"Sure," she said, gesturing him into the living room. "Would you like some tea or something? Bea's in the kitchen as we speak, and—"

"No, I'm fine," he told her, then followed her to the sofa.

He looked down at Chloe decimating the coloring book and the anger seemed to melt away. He smiled. "I see she's got her mother's talent for art."

Lisa laughed. "I'm afraid so."

The memory he'd invoked was a warm one. In college Lisa had taken several art classes but was woefully bad at every single one of them—a running joke in their relationship. For a while he had called her Picasso, a good-natured dig and a term of endearment.

That was something she had always cherished back then. His affection. He gave it freely and without expecting anything in return. Especially in bed. He was the most attentive man she had ever been with, and she still remembered, with great clarity, their nights together.

Ah, but that was then and this is now. And while she felt a certain warmth from Rafe, there was also a reserved, almost professional politeness to it. Something he had no doubt learned on the job.

She watched as he crouched next to Chloe and seemed to take great interest in her task.

"What're you coloring there, kiddo?"

Chloe barely looked up at him. She wasn't normally a shy child, but she was too busy working her blue crayon to be bothered with some stranger in a uniform.

"A kitty cat," she murmured.

"A kitty cat with blue fur," Rafe said. "I like it. I wish I could have one just like that in my apartment."

She looked up at him now, and as Lisa watched, her heart was breaking.

Tell him, you idiot.

Tell him.

"You can have this one, if you want," Chloe said. "He's almost done."

"Are you sure?" Rafe asked. "I wouldn't want you to miss him. And he might get lonely at my place."

Chloe seemed confused for a moment, then squinted at him. "Do you live all by yourself?"

"I'm afraid I do, kiddo."

"Then you can be friends and he can live with you," she said, then went back to coloring.

Rafe smiled again, tousled her head, then

got to his feet, turning to Lisa. "Where were we?"

Trying to keep from bursting into tears, Lisa thought.

She said, "I'm not sure. You wanted to talk about Oliver?"

Rafe nodded solemnly. "I'm afraid things didn't go as well as I hoped they would. In fact, it was a disaster. Your ex isn't exactly an agreeable man."

"I'm pretty sure I warned you about that. Did he try to hurt you?"

"I only wish he had. I might've been able to make the charges against him stick."

"Charges? What charges?"

Rafe told her about his early-morning confrontation with Oliver, about the woman in Oliver's bed, the bag of cocaine, the arrest and court, and by the time he was done, Lisa's head was whirling.

But she wasn't surprised by any of it.

Nothing about Oliver surprised her anymore. She just wished he was out of her life for good.

"So why are you here?" she asked. "To warn me?"

"Emphatically," Rafe said. "I got the distinct impression that Sloan is not happy with you right now, and I'd bet a year's salary that he'll be back here, late one night. And you may not be able to get rid of him this time."

A feeling of dread worked its way through Lisa's bloodstream. "You think I'm not safe here?"

"Not in the least," Rafe said. "I think you should pack some things and get out. You, your daughter and your housekeeper. As soon as you possibly can."

"But where will we go? A hotel?"

"I wouldn't advise that. As I told you, your ex has some very powerful associates and they'd undoubtedly find you at a hotel."

Something caught his eye and he reached to the end table and picked up the photograph Oliver had shattered when he broke into the house. The one with her and Chloe standing in front of the lake house.

"Nice photo," he said. "What about this place? Looks like Carlyle Lake."

She nodded. "We spent a lot of time there before we moved to St. Louis."

"A rental?"

She shook her head. "No, it's Oliver's. He kept it in the divorce settlement. He's pretty attached to the place. I think because it was the only time in our marriage that we were actually happy."

"Scratch that idea, then." He set the photo back down. Then he said, "You remember back in college, when we came out here for the weekend?"

She nodded, the pictures flooding her mind. "We stayed at your grandmother's house."

"That's right. Grandma Natalie. That house is way too big for her now, and she's all alone, so I'm sure she'd be happy to have the company."

"I wouldn't want to impose," Lisa said.

He shook his head. "Don't worry, I'm her favorite grandson. She'll be more than happy to do me the favor."

Lisa nodded again, thinking that if she could get Rafe alone in that big house, sharing a bit of quiet time as they'd had during that visit many years ago, she might be able to level with him. Tell him the truth about Chloe.

Assuming she could work up the nerve.

"All right," she said. "We'll start packing right away."

"Good. I've been up all night, so I'm gonna

go catch a quick nap and I'll be back to pick you up early this evening. Will that work?"

"Of course."

"And if Sloan shows up on your doorstep again, tell your housekeeper not to hesitate to pull the trigger this time."

A FEW MOMENTS LATER, Rafe drove toward his apartment, but soon realized he was much too wired to take a nap.

As he had stood in Lisa's house again, had knelt next to her beautiful little daughter, Undersheriff Macon's demand kept running through his head.

It's simple. We want you to turn her.

We want you to nurture the relationship and convince her to be our confidential informant.

Rafe could fully understand why they'd want to use Lisa to spy on Sloan, but he would never allow it. He'd never put her in a position of danger like that. His job was to protect people like Lisa, not throw them to the wolves.

It was one thing to bust a criminal and make him your confidential informant in exchange for leniency or a free pass. But Lisa was an innocent. A woman who had met the wrong guy and fallen for his ruse. It would be heartless to use that mistake against her, even if it meant bringing Sloan's criminal enterprise to its knees.

And there was no guarantee of that. Sloan was dangerous enough to Lisa as it was. If he were to somehow find out that she was working with the Sheriff's department, he might very well kill her.

Or keep his hands clean and have her killed.

So the thought that Rafe would ever try to turn Lisa was insulting and ridiculous, and it annoyed him that his sister Kate had asked him to take a couple days to think about it. Even the carrot she'd dangled—a promotion to Homicide—wouldn't make him change his mind.

After seeing Lisa today, still as lovely and alluring as she had been in college, all thoughts of his career had abruptly vanished. Worrying about a promotion suddenly seemed so unimportant to him that he couldn't believe he'd been fretting about it.

He couldn't stop thinking about Lisa and his last days with her, that moment when he knew she was afraid to commit and was looking for a way out of their relationship.

He had made up all those stories about wanting to go to California and be a surf bum, because he was trying to let her off the hook. He'd pretended that he, too, wanted to explore options, but his only *real* desire had been for them to stay together. Instead he'd done what he thought would make her happy. Had even headed out West after graduation—a pointless exercise if there ever was one.

He had all but convinced himself that he'd never see her again—and that she had no desire to see *him*—until he walked into her living room.

It had been a struggle to maintain his distance. To remain professional. Yet despite the facade, he'd felt more attracted to her than ever. He'd even felt an instant and unexpected connection to her daughter, Chloe, who was, quite possibly, the cutest kid he'd ever seen.

Before he left, Chloe had carefully torn the page with the blue cat out of her coloring book and handed it to him. And in that moment, Rafe felt an inexplicable hitch in his throat. Something about the child had gotten to him, very quickly, and he was touched by her generosity.

She certainly hadn't inherited this from her father.

Maybe what Rafe had felt was the power of his regret welling up on him. His failure to fight for Lisa rather than let her go. Her daughter, Chloe, was a kind of symbol of that regret. She was what *could have been.*

Had he and Lisa stayed together, Chloe— or someone very much like her—could have been his child.

But fate has a way of throwing curveballs at you, and Rafe knew that what was done was done.

As he drove toward his apartment, however, a thought occurred to him. If he could get Lisa and Chloe squared away, if he could get a toxic presence like Sloan out of their lives forever…maybe he and Lisa could rediscover what they once had.

And maybe, just maybe, he could call that little girl his own.

Chapter Fourteen

Rafe had nearly reached his apartment house when he suddenly remembered something: the receipt he'd picked up in the Jaguar this morning. The one he'd found near the dead driver's foot.

If, as Kate suspected, those two hits were the handiwork of Oliver Sloan, maybe Rafe could find a way to pin it on the guy and send him away forever.

Assuming the brass would let him.

Such a move might not topple an entire criminal network, but Rafe frankly wasn't concerned about that. His only interest at this point was in helping Lisa. Though he'd already gotten himself into trouble with the department by going rogue this morning, he didn't figure another trip off the rails could hurt him that much.

And he was more than happy to sacrifice his job to protect Lisa.

He had no idea if Kate and her crew had yet identified the dead Russians. But he had every intention of checking into it himself.

Suddenly energized, he dug into his jacket pocket and pulled out the receipt. According to the time stamp, the gas had been pumped at approximately 2:45 a.m. at a service station on Davis. There was no indication whether or not the customer had paid cash or used a credit card, but there was a way to find out.

It might amount to nothing, but he had to try.

Shifting his Mustang into gear, Rafe hit the accelerator, made a wide, squealing U-turn and headed across town.

THE DAVIS STREET service station was your typical low-end franchise that boasted nine pumps, a repair garage and snack shop about the size of Rafe's living room.

The pumps looked as if they hadn't been replaced or refurbished in ten years, but the gas was cheap and the snack shop served cherry super slushes.

So maybe the place wasn't all that bad.

The guy behind the counter wasn't a week past sixteen and carried the scruffy aura of a high school dropout. He glanced up nervously as Rafe, still in his uniform, stepped inside and dug the receipt out of his pocket.

"Your supervisor around?"

The kid was staring at the Glock holstered on Rafe's hip. "Huh?"

"Your boss. Is he on the premises?"

"Uh, no, he only shows up for a couple hours in the morning. He's gone for the day."

Rafe had no idea if this kid would have the wherewithal to help him, but figured if there were any questions, he'd be a lot easier to manipulate than the guy who owned this franchise.

He put the receipt on the counter.

"I'm investigating a homicide," he said. "The guy who was killed bought gas here this morning at 2:45."

"No kidding?"

"No kidding," Rafe said. "I need to know what he used to pay for the gas. Is there any way to check that?"

The kid hesitated. "Aren't you supposed to have, like, a warrant or something?"

"I'm not asking for his hospital records," Rafe said. "Just a simple gas purchase. Can you give me that?"

The kid scratched his head, a mop that looked as if it hadn't been washed within the past week or so, and was undoubtedly full of lice, then gestured to the register in front of him, which was part calculator, part personal computer, complete with a flat-screen display.

"It should be in here," he said. "If the thing didn't crash, like it does every other transaction."

Transaction seemed like a big word for him, but he'd managed to get it out.

Rafe said, "Well, why don't you take a look at that receipt, then do what you have to do to find out."

"Okay..."

The kid picked up the piece of paper, squinted at it, then slowly began punching in a string of numbers on the register keyboard. After a moment, the computer bleeped and something came up on screen.

"It was paid for with a debit card by a guy named...Serge..." He squinted at the screen now, and Rafe could see he was having trouble trying to figure out how to pronounce the customer's last name.

"Just spell it for me," Rafe said.

The kid did as he was told and Rafe took one of the station's business cards from a holder, then used a pen next to the register to write the name on the back.

Serge Azarov.

When he was done, he noticed the kid was looking at his Glock again. "You ever use that thing?"

"It's been known to happen," Rafe said.

"You ever kill anyone?"

"Once."

The kid's eyes lit up. "Yeah? Who?"

"A guy about your age, as a matter of fact."

The kid swallowed. "Really? What'd he do?"

"He dropped out of high school," Rafe said.

RAFE ACCESSED the LAWCOM database with his smartphone. The only Serge Azarov listed was a forty-two-year-old, two-time offender, who had been busted on a weapons charge four years ago, and had only recently been released from jail.

His photo matched the face of the dead driver.

Since his release, he'd taken up residence is a run-down apartment house in a notorious section of a city that was already considered by some to be one of the most dangerous in the world.

Rafe had seen a lot of violence in St. Louis, and the city certainly had its share of troubles, but statistics also had a way of skewing people's perception of the world, and he thought much of that perception was colored by paranoia.

That didn't keep him from remaining very alert as he entered the neighborhood Serge Azarov had called home. And because he had to assume that Kate and her partner might also be looking for this guy, Rafe had decided to park his Mustang a few blocks away, chuck his uniform into the trunk, and change into the jeans, T-shirt and hoodie he kept stored there.

The last thing he needed was nosy neighbors ratting him out to Eberhart and his sister.

He stuck his Glock in the waistband of his pants, near the small of his back, then put his hood up and walked to the apartment house, which was a ratty, ten-story walk-up with graffiti-stained, wrought-iron bars protecting the lobby door.

He punched a bunch of buttons on the security com until someone finally buzzed him in, then climbed two flights of stairs to a corridor dotted with doors. He could hear a couple screaming at each other at the far end of the hall, and a baby crying just two doors away.

Rafe found apartment 211, and rapped his

knuckles against the door, hoping Azarov had lived alone.

The was no answer. A good sign. And after a couple more tries no one came to the door.

Rafe pulled out his wallet, and removed the slender lock picks he kept tucked inside it. He was about to lean forward and go to work, when a door down the hall flew open and an elderly woman in a bathrobe looked out at him.

"You look for Serge?" she said in thick Russian accent.

Rafe turned his head slightly, but didn't look directly at her, hoping the hoodie would give him some protection. He didn't need anyone seeing his face, just in case things went south. "Yes, ma'am. I'm a friend of his."

"Serge no home," she said. "He supposed to have breakfast with his aunt Luba, but he no show."

Small wonder, Rafe thought. "Do you have any idea when he'll be back?"

She eyed him suspiciously. "What you want from him?"

Rafe took a chance. "He borrowed one of my tools and I need it to fix my car."

"Here," the woman said, then disappeared inside. She came back, holding a set of keys, then shuffled toward the doorway. "I let you in to get it."

She shot Rafe a look as she approached and he backed up to give her room. He couldn't avoid her gaze this time.

"I can trust you?" she said.

"Yes, ma'am, of course."

"Not all Serge's friends are good boys. Sometimes even Serge isn't a good—"

A phone rang, the sound coming from her open doorway. The woman looked startled, then quickly handed Rafe the keys. "That might be him now," she said. "You bring them back when you finish."

"Yes, ma'am," Rafe told her, and watched her shuffle off the way she came.

Letting out a breath, he found the right key, then opened the door and stepped inside, buffeted by the strong stench of cigarettes. He closed the door behind him and locked it, just in case the old woman came back.

The place was early dump, with a threadbare carpet and walls that featured tobacco-stained, flowered wallpaper that looked as if it had been installed sometime in the fifties. It was a one-bedroom unit, with a simple sofa, chair and television in the living room, with an attached kitchenette.

There was an abandoned, drying bowl of cereal on the coffee table, an ashtray full of Russian cigarette butts—the source of the stench—and a jacket draped over the couch. Rafe picked it up and rifled through the pockets but found nothing.

He wasn't really quite sure what he was looking for. Something that might tell him who Azarov's friends and associates were. But the guy didn't seem to have lived here long, which made sense, considering he'd only recently been released from prison.

Rafe went to the kitchenette and rifled through the drawers and cabinets, but all he found were a few chipped dishes and some tarnished silverware that should have been replaced a decade ago.

Rafe knew that if he didn't take these keys back soon, Aunt Luba was likely to come snooping. Kicking into higher gear, he headed into the bedroom and found an unmade twin bed covered with a stained flat sheet and ratty blankets, butted up against the wall next to a window with a fire escape.

The closet was hanging open and bare except for a couple more jackets, which Rafe quickly searched.

Nothing.

A battered dresser stood in a corner and he yanked open the drawers, finding nothing but a few pairs of underwear, three T-shirts and two pairs of socks. No receipts, no photographs, no letters—nothing.

In other words, this was big fat waste of time.

Rafe was turning toward the bedroom door when he heard muffled voices in the hallway.

"I tell him to bring them back when he finish," Aunt Luba was saying, "But he no come. He must still be in here."

"You have any idea who this guy is?" another voice said, and at the sound of it, Rafe's heart stopped.

It was Eberhart. And Kate was undoubtedly with him.

Uh-oh.

"Do you have another set of keys?" Eberhart asked.

"No," Aunt Luba told him.

The small apartment suddenly filled with the sound of pounding, fist on wood, the door rattling loudly with every jolt. "Sheriff's department! Open up in there!"

Rafe stood frozen in place, knowing he was toast, knowing that this was likely the end of his job, and despite all his self-proclamations earlier, he wasn't quite ready to give up on it. Not just yet.

And as he heard the pounding on the door again, Eberhart shouting for him to open up, he knew that the next sound would be splintering wood.

Rafe didn't think, just reacted. Turning on his heels, he launched himself toward the window with the fire escape.

He was across the room in three strides, hands grabbing for the lock, struggling to push the window open, when the inevitable happened behind him, the front door crashing wide, as Eberhart and Kate entered the premises.

Mostly likely with guns drawn.

Rafe yanked at the window, trying to force it open, and finally, thankfully, it scraped upward, just enough for him to squeeze through—

And a sound just loud enough to be heard in the living room.

He dove through it just as Kate shouted behind him, "Police! Stop!"

But Rafe didn't stop, didn't slow down. He scrambled onto the fire escape and started his descent, glad that the window was dirty and that his face was obscured by the hoodie.

Fortunately, he was only two flights up and it took him no time at all to navigate the steps and leap to the blacktop below.

He stood in the alleyway at the rear of the building, heard footsteps clanging on the metal above him, Kate once again shouting for him to halt.

"You! Stop right there!"

He took off running, heading for the mouth of the alley, a sudden sense of guilt sweeping through him—he was running from his own *sister*—but he couldn't risk being caught.

Kate kept shouting and he could tell by the sound of her voice that she was working her way down the fire escape. He hit the mouth of the alley and turned, picking up speed, but he'd run plenty of races with Kate as a kid and he knew just how fast she was.

A moment later he heard her shouting again as she came around the corner behind him. Rafe suddenly flashed back to early this morning when he was chasing the suspect at the auto repair shop and it was hard for him to believe he was now on the receiving end of such a chase.

He bore down again and picked up speed, his lungs drawing in ragged breaths. Kate had stopped shouting and he knew she was now concentrating on breathing and quite possibly gaining on him. But he couldn't look back. He didn't want her to recognize him.

Rafe reached the end of a street, darted across the intersection, nearly colliding with a car that had sped up to jump a red light, then shot across to another alleyway, hoping that Kate had been slowed at the intersection.

But a moment later, she shouted again, struggling to breathe herself, and he knew she was much too close for comfort. "Stop! Stop right now!"

Rafe almost expected her to call out his name, because surely she must recognize him even from behind, but he didn't waste time worrying about it. He put the hammer to the pedal and picked up even more speed, heading toward a pair of metal doors in the side of the building.

One of them was ajar.

"Stop!" Kate shouted once again, and he could tell by the faltering tone that she was starting to get winded, losing speed.

Rafe reached the doors and launched himself against them, flinging them open to reveal nothing but darkness inside. This was a warehouse of some kind or a storage facility.

As he got inside, he kept moving through

the darkness, waiting for his eyes to adjust and hoping he wouldn't bump into anything. After a moment, it became clear that this was a file depot of some sort, the massive place crowded with numbered legal boxes sitting on low rows of shelves.

Rafe could hear Kate's footsteps behind him. She would be inside at any moment now and, per protocol, would slow herself down and draw her weapon.

He wondered for a moment if he should just give this up and cop to the truth, but there was a large part of him that resisted for one simple reason—he didn't want to look like a complete fool in front of his older sister. Rafe had spent his entire childhood trying to impress both Kate and their older brother, Vincent. And he knew Kate would not react well if she discovered the man she was chasing was her own kid brother.

So he kept moving, working his way through the rows of shelves, looking for another door. A way out.

He saw one on the far side of the second row he entered, visible mostly because of the light seeping under the door. He abruptly shifted direction and was halfway to it when Kate shouted, "Freeze!"

A flashlight beam illuminated Rafe's back, throwing his elongated shadow onto the floor and up onto the boxes.

Rafe stopped in his tracks, raised his arms and knew what was coming.

"Down on your knees!" Kate commanded.

Rafe's heart was thumping in his ears.

Oh, well, he thought. *At least I tried.*

He was about to drop to his knees when another voice shouted, "What is this? What's going on here?"

Rafe recognized the indignant, authoritative tone of what had to be the building security guard, probably pulling his own weapon from his holster as he spoke.

Rafe froze in place, knew that Kate would have to respond, and she did immediately. He also knew that she'd be showing the guard her weapon in a nonthreatening manner to keep him from firing his own.

"County Sheriff, sir! Don't fire. Do not—"

That was when Rafe bolted. Made a bee-line straight for the door, Kate again shouting for him to halt or she'd shoot. But he didn't falter, didn't slow down, knowing that she would aim for his legs.

He zigged and zagged and the first shot didn't ring out until he reached the door,

gouging the floor nearby. It ricocheted harm-
lessly, just as he slammed through the door
and burst onto the street, once again running
for all he was worth.

Rafe had a better lead on her this time and
he wasn't about to let himself get caught. His
lungs felt shallow, each breath harder than
the next, but he didn't let it slow him down,
couldn't let it.

He took a right at the next block, then
darted across the street, ran to the next corner and took a left, finally chancing a look
behind him.

No sign of Kate. Or Eberhart, wherever
he'd gone to. Probably still back at Azarov's
apartment, relaxing and smoking a cigarette.

Rafe took two more turns, left, then right,
then stripped off the hoodie and dumped it
into a trash can on the street. Crossing the
next intersection, he spotted a coffee shop
and went inside, finding a booth in back that
allowed him a view of the street.

A waitress nodded to him as he slid into the
booth, gave him a small smile and he smiled
back, even though he didn't much feel it.

He sat there trying to catch his breath, then
gestured for the waitress to bring him a cup
of coffee.

He waited in the booth for nearly an hour before going back to Azarov's neighborhood to retrieve his Mustang.

Chapter Fifteen

"Are you sure this'll be okay with your grand-mother?"

"I've already called her," Rafe said. "She's more than happy to have the company. Thrilled, in fact."

They were driving at a clip in Rafe's Mustang, Lisa up front next to him, Chloe and Bea in back. Lisa felt uncomfortable and nervous, but wasn't really sure why. She had met Grandma Natalie during her junior year, when Rafe had brought Lisa home for the weekend.

Maybe the nerves were caused by the way Rafe was driving, which was a tad too fast for her. When he had shown up at the door look-ing disheveled in jeans and a T-shirt—as if he had just returned from a jog at the park—she'd had to wonder what he'd been up to.

She was immediately reminded of how gor-geous he was, but he seemed distracted and a little out of sorts. Something was weighing on his mind.

Maybe some of that had rubbed off on her.

Or maybe her nerves were simply caused by the secret she knew she had to reveal. The one sitting right there in the backseat, playing Crazy Birds on an iPad.

The closer they got to Grandma Natalie's house, the more trepidation Lisa felt. She had spent half the day wondering how she would break the news to Rafe, and still hadn't come up with an idea that would guarantee a happy outcome.

But then she supposed nothing could.

This feeling was compounded by her mixed emotions about Rafe himself. He had only been back in her life for a few short hours—and only a small portion of *that,* when she thought about it—yet she felt as if something had been awakened inside her. Some long-abandoned emotion that had lain dormant, quietly percolating below the surface of her heart for the past three years.

Why, she wondered, did it matter to her how he reacted to the news about Chloe?

Was she still in love with him?

After everything she had been through with Oliver, was she still even capable of love?

All she knew was that, despite the turmoil inside her, she felt good being with Rafe again, riding beside him in this Mustang that he'd had for so many years. It was the same car they drove here as juniors, and she felt at home in it. Just as she had back then.

She felt safe with him, protected.

It was the role Rafe had always taken. Lisa had grown up very much the independent woman, but when she'd met Rafe in her freshman year—or the tall, reedy teenager he was back then—she had quickly discovered that she didn't mind his old-fashioned, chivalrous ways. He opened doors for her, pulled out chairs for her, gave her his coat if they were caught in the rain, stood up to boys who made drunken passes at her at frat parties or disparaging remarks when she turned them down.

Yet he did all this without ever robbing her of her independence. Without ever undermining the essence of who she was as a woman.

Now he here was again, falling so easily into the old role. Looking out for her. Helping her.

He was staring intently at the road as he drove and she wanted so much to ask him what he was thinking about right now.

"You seem preoccupied," she said. "Is something wrong?"

He shook his head. "Nothing I can't handle."

"Does it have something to do with Oliver?"

He glanced at her, smiled. "Don't you worry about that jerk. He's my number-one case now."

"Meaning what?"

"That sooner or later I'm gonna find a way to put him behind bars, where he belongs."

Lisa shook her head. "I still can't believe all this stuff about his being involved in organized crime. I mean the mob?"

"This isn't like the old days, Lisa. Gangsters don't dress up like the godfather or threaten people with tommy guns. Organized crime is fronted and populated by people who look like legitimate businessmen, and are often so far removed from the actual wrongdoing that it's nearly impossible to put them away."

"So then what makes you think you'll be able to do anything about Oliver?" she asked.

"Determination," he said. "Pure determination."

GRANDMA NATALIE LIVED on the Hill, a largely Italian-American neighborhood marked by the brick and terra-cotta Roman Catholic church that stood on the corner of Wilson and Marconi Avenues.

The house itself was a two-story, red-and-white, bungalow-style affair with a large front porch overlooking Shaw Avenue, which was fairly busy at this time of day.

Rafe pulled the Mustang into the drive, and before they even had their doors all the way open, Grandma Natalie emerged from the front doorway—looking just as Lisa remembered her—arms extended to Rafe.

She was a small, plump Italian woman in her mid- eighties, with a smile that was big and wide and friendly.

Lisa watched as Rafe went to the foot of the porch and pulled her into a hug.

"Rafael," the old woman sang. "My sweet little Rafael."

Not so little anymore, Lisa thought. He dwarfed the old woman.

"Good to see you, Nonna. How've you been?"

"I work, I eat, I sleep," she said. "Then I start all over again." She pulled away and held him at arm's length, studying him. "You look tired, Rafael. Have you been sleeping?"

He shook his head. "I never made it home after my shift," he told her. "I'm pretty beat."

"Well, come then. Come sit inside in your grandfather's chair and take a nap. I'll make some tea and keep your friends company."

This was Rafe's cue to turn to Lisa, Bea and Chloe. "Nonna, you remember Lisa, don't you?"

Now the old woman turned her smile on them, and in that moment Lisa could swear she felt warmth flowing through her. Almost magical in its energy.

"Ah, yes," Grandma Natalie said, taking Lisa's hands in hers. "Of course I remember. The one who got away."

Lisa and Rafe exchanged a brief glance, an embarrassed smile, then Rafe gestured to Bea and Chloe and introduced them.

Natalie nodded to Bea, then stooped toward Chloe, reaching a hand out to tousle her hair. "What a beautiful little…"

She paused, a question forming in her eyes.

She glanced up at Lisa, then Rafe, then at Lisa again, who quickly averted her gaze. Rafe didn't seem to notice the look, but in that moment, Lisa knew that the old woman had seen something familiar in Chloe. Probably the same thing Lisa saw every time she looked at her daughter's face.

Rafael Franco's eyes.

"Lovely child," the old woman said. "Let's see if we can find you some cookies."

Chloe's face lit up. "Really?"

"As long as your mama approves."

Lisa smiled. "Of course. Thank you so much for having us, Mrs. Franco."

"Call me Nonna," she said, then lightly flicked a finger under Chloe's chin, provoking a giggle. "You, too."

"Okay."

Then she straightened and turned to Rafe. "Rafael, don't just stand there looking handsome. Get their things and carry them to their rooms upstairs. I'll start the tea."

THE INTERIOR of the house was a museum. A perfectly maintained replica of 1920s St. Louis, with antique furniture, polished wood floors and a gleaming wooden staircase that led to the bedrooms.

Lisa had forgotten that feeling she'd had so long ago, when she had first stepped foot inside the house. It seemed to hold the same welcoming warmth as Grandma Natalie's smile. A house that said, *Come in, come in. Make yourself comfortable.*

"I remember the first moment I saw you," Nonna said to her as she poured tea into delicate porcelain cups.

They were seated in the large but intimate living room, the air so still that every clink of the porcelain seemed magnified.

"I was in the kitchen," she continued, "with the window overlooking the drive, and Rafael drove up in that infernal machine of his, and a moment later you stepped out." She smiled. "I thought, oh, my, what has that grandson of mine gone and done?"

Rafe, who was slumped wearily in a worn leather chair, cracked open his eyes and said, "What's that supposed to mean, Nonna?"

"That as handsome and charming as you are, young man, I couldn't quite believe you had managed to steal such a beautiful treasure. Especially after some of the ungodly young women you dated in high school."

Bea, who looked a little uncomfortable being served, let out a snort. "I like this woman."

Nonna smiled at her. "I'll bet you'll like my lasagna even better. Just you wait and see."

"Come on, Nonna," Rafe said. "Cut me a break."

The old woman ignored him and turned again to Lisa. "And when I met you, I was quite delighted that he'd finally managed to find someone who was not only beautiful, but also had brains, too. Rafael's a wonderful boy, but he doesn't always think straight. He needs to be grounded in reality sometimes and you seemed like just the woman to do it."

Rafe sat up now, blinking at her. "How long are you planning to go on like this?"

"You just go to sleep, son. Let the ladies talk."

"I feel like I'm under a microscope."

Nonna waggled a hand at him. "Just be happy anyone's talking about you at all. You could do worse."

Rafe gave her a good-natured scowl, then settled back in his seat and closed his eyes. "I couldn't stop you if I wanted to, so carry on."

"Boys and their grandmothers," Bea murmured with a grin.

Nonna finished pouring her own cup of tea, stirred in some sugar, then settled onto the sofa, again addressing Lisa.

"Where was I?" she asked.

"Talking about how Rafe needs grounding," Lisa said, more concerned about where the old woman was *going* with all this. During the entire monologue she had kept glancing at Chloe, who was once again in deep communion with her crayons.

"Ah, yes," Nonna said. "So you'll understand why I was surprised and disappointed when the two of you broke it off. I had gotten the impression that Rafe was quite enamored of you, and you of him."

Rafe opened his eyes again. "Okay, Nonna, now you're really pushing it. Time to change the subject."

She glanced at Chloe again. "A grandmother can't be concerned about the choices her grandson makes? Especially when he may have certain responsibilities…"

Rafe frowned. "What the heck are you talking about?"

Lisa knew exactly what the old woman's concern was and she immediately moved to allay it. "The breakup was a mutual decision, Nonna. And it didn't come easily." She smiled. "I'm just happy we've had this chance to reconnect, even if it's under unfortunate circumstances."

Grandma Natalie looked at her. "Then I take it he doesn't…"

She stopped, letting the unspoken question hang in the air, and Lisa felt a sharp, painful stab of guilt.

"Doesn't what?" Rafe asked.

Lisa looked directly at the old woman, mentally imploring her not to go any further. She didn't want Rafe to find out like this.

"Nonna?"

The message seemed to get through, as Nonna relaxed. "Never you mind, son, you're half asleep. You'd better take that nap before dinner. The stomach won't wait."

Rafe studied her curiously for a moment, glanced at Lisa, then threw his hands up in an exasperated gesture that implied that women were a mystery to him.

Then he closed his eyes again.

Chapter Sixteen

Dinner crept up on them faster than anyone had expected. Chloe unpacked the toys she brought in the living room as Lisa and Bea helped Grandma Natalie in the kitchen and a still-groggy Rafe set the dining room table.

Lisa remembered what a wonderful cook Grandma Natalie was. One Sunday every month, the entire Franco clan gathered here at the house to break bread and catch up with one another. Grandma Natalie would prepare a feast and the wine flowed as if it were coming from a fountain in the floor.

Lisa had been part of one of those Sundays. Had met Rafe's brother, Vincent, and his aunts and uncles and cousins, all of whom seemed to have some connection to firefighting or law enforcement. Sheriff's deputies, firefighters, beat cops, detectives, arson investigators. The Franco family was permeated by the culture and seemed to revel in it.

On the drive in, back then, Rafe had warned Lisa that she was about to be surrounded by some of the toughest cops she had ever encountered—not that she had encountered many—and that she shouldn't let them intimidate her. That they were loyal to the badge, but they were also good people. Compassionate people.

"My family," he had told her, "lives and breathes by our own code."

"Code?"

"It's based on what's informally called Code Blue, the police code of conduct."

"Sounds a little ominous to me," she had said.

Rafe shook his head. "Just the opposite. Since childhood, I've always been taught by example to respect others, show empathy and humanity, do no harm unless it's justified, protect those who can't protect themselves, trust and help one another when needed... and..."

"And what?"

"Avoid bringing shame on the family. I know it all sounds a little goody-goody, but it works for us."

At the time, Lisa had thought this code painted a vivid portrait of the Rafe she knew.

He had always been a man—a boy then, really—of integrity, who seemed very sure about who he was and what he believed in. Cop confidence was part of his DNA, but never in that annoying, holier-than-thou way demonstrated by so many of the campus police officers.

Rafe was the picture of solid, but gentle, self-assurance. A picture Lisa had found quite attractive.

Still did.

Not that Rafe didn't have his doubts at times. He had often told her about his reluctance to follow in his siblings' footsteps and join the force. But that had come more from a fear of disappointing them than anything else. He was afraid he wouldn't live up to the Franco family name.

He was especially concerned about living up to the example set by his sister, Kate—whom Lisa hadn't met that Sunday. She was apparently one of the shining stars of the Franco family and Rafe said he often felt inadequate around her.

But now it looked as if he had finally conquered that fear and had grown and matured since making his decision to join the department. And helping her with Oliver proved that he still lived by the credo the Francos so cherished.

It was the last part of it, however, that bothered her.

Avoid bringing shame on the family.

These were modern times, sure, but the Franco clan struck her as a bit old-fashioned. So would the news that one of their favorite sons had fathered a child out of wedlock be greeted as a source of shame, or of celebration?

It was probably a pointless worry, but such things weighed on Lisa's mind. Especially when the matriarch of that family was busy making pasta primavera right next to her, and knew darn well that the little girl now helping Rafe set the table was her great-granddaughter.

Lisa ached inside, knowing she needed to tell Rafe the truth, but still unable to think of a way—or a time—to do it.

But it had to be done.

No matter what the consequences.

DINNER WAS SUBLIME. Lisa couldn't remember the last time she'd had food so delicious.

Grandma Natalie was an amazing cook.

They ate for what seemed like hours, sharing a bottle of wine, Rafe forgoing a glass because he had to work a shift tonight. Somewhere in the middle of it all, Chloe began to yawn and Lisa decided it was time to put her to bed.

"Let's get you upstairs, hon. You've got to wash up and change into your jammies."

"Can Mr. Rafe take me?"

This provoked a smile. "I don't see why not," Rafe said. "But none of this mister, stuff. Just call me Rafe."

Or Daddy, Lisa almost blurted out, but caught herself just in time. And she half expected Grandma Natalie to say it instead.

Getting to her feet, Lisa said, "We'll both do it, hon. Make it a party."

"A party!" Chloe squealed. "Make it party!"

"How about a teeth-brushing contest?" Rafe asked.

"Yea!" Chloe squealed.

Laughing, Rafe got to his feet, then went around the table and scooped Chloe into his arms. "I'll bet I can get mine cleaner than yours."

"Uh-uh," Chloe said.

"We'll see about that," Rafe chuckled, then carried her out of the dining room toward the stairs.

Laughing now, Lisa got to her feet and followed, but before she reached the doorway, Grandma Natalie called out to her.

Lisa turned. "Yes?"

"You may not think this is any of my business, child, but does my grandson know who he's carrying upstairs?"

Lisa's laugh died and she said, "He will soon, Nonna. I promise. Just as soon as I figure out a way to tell him."

Beatrice frowned. "Tell him what? Am I missing something?"

Grandma Natalie patiently patted Bea's hand and returned her attention to Lisa. "Just open your mouth and say the words, child. That's all it takes."

Knowing the old woman was right, Lisa nodded solemnly then headed toward the stairs.

Chapter Seventeen

"I made something for you," Chloe said.

Rafe smiled. "Oh? What is it?"

He was crouched over the bed in what had once been his mother's bedroom, a small space located near the back of the house. The window overlooked the backyard where Mom's old swing set still stood, victim to a bit of rot and rust, but gleaming in the moonlight, an old, pleasant memory.

Rafe had spent quite a bit of time on those swings himself.

He pulled the blankets up toward Chloe's chin as she said, "It's in my backpack."

Rafe glanced at Lisa, who stood leaning in the doorway, watching them. There was a look in her eyes that puzzled him. A vague sadness, he thought. Something bothering her.

Undoubtedly thoughts of Sloan. It had to be hard raising a man's child when that very same man was a threat to you. She undoubtedly saw part of Sloan every time she looked at Chloe's face.

Rafe didn't see it, however. He couldn't bring himself to equate this precious child with Oliver Sloan. She was too innocent, too…beautiful.

Her mother's beauty, he supposed.

It certainly wasn't Sloan's.

"Are you gonna look at it?" Chloe asked.

Rafe snapped out of his thoughts and reached for the backpack hanging over the bedpost—a lime-green frog with more zippered pockets than anyone could ever need, especially a child.

"In here?"

"Uh-huh."

Rafe unzipped the main pocket and reached inside, pulling out a sheet of paper that had been torn from a coloring book. It was another kitty cat. This one crudely colored pink.

"Do you like it?" Chloe asked.

"I love it," he said. "But you already gave me a blue one." Which, he realized, was still folded in the pocket of his uniform jacket in the trunk of his car.

"You said you didn't want him to get lonely, so I made him a friend."

For reasons he couldn't quite understand, Rafe felt a sudden warmth sluice through him. This was, quite possibly, one of the most heartfelt things anyone had ever done for him.

He again felt that unexplained connection to this little girl, and his chest filled with a yearning that came very close to bringing on tears.

He held back. Smiled. Ran a hand along Chloe's forehead. "Thank you, hon. This is the best present anyone ever gave me."

"Really?"

"Absolutely," Rafe said. Then he heard a quiet sob behind him and swiveled his head to find Lisa turning quickly away from the doorway, heading into the hall.

"Leese?"

She didn't respond and he felt compelled to go after her, but didn't want to leave Chloe in a lurch. Instead, he turned back to the girl, smoothed her forehead again, and said, "You'd better get to sleep now, cupcake."

Chloe smiled. "I like cupcakes."

"So do I," Rafe said. "So do I."

HE FOUND LISA on the front porch, sitting on the swinging bench that his grandfather had built. The old man had been very proud of that accomplishment. He was a gruff old patrol cop who hated retirement and always had to be doing something with his hands. His death two years ago had been a deep blow to everyone in the family.

Rafe remembered how Lisa had spent a lot of time on this bench the weekend he'd brought her here during college. The Franco clan could be an overwhelming bunch and although she had never admitted it, Rafe sensed that her weekend among them had been plagued by sensory overload.

While Rafe was busy having fun catching up with family, Lisa had been a stranger in a strange land, and that couldn't have been easy for her. So it wasn't surprising that she'd spent time out here, trying to gather her thoughts.

And he supposed tonight wasn't any different. She'd been uprooted and moved out of her house and had to be feeling the stress of her situation. He didn't know what had triggered her sudden retreat from the bedroom, but he found himself falling into his old rhythms with Lisa, wanting to comfort and protect her.

He sat next to her on the swing, saw that she had a trace of tears in her eyes.

They hadn't had physical contact except

for the hug this morning, and right now Rafe wanted to put his arm around her and pull her close.

But he resisted.

"It wasn't that long ago," he said. "You and me sitting here on a night like this, looking up at the sky. Yet it seems like some faded childhood dream."

Lisa nodded, wiped at her tears. "Were we really as in love as we thought we were?"

Rafe thought about this, but didn't really need to. He already knew the answer. "I know *I* was."

She smiled wistfully. Nodded. "Then what happened, Rafe? Why did we go our separate ways?"

"I've thought a lot about that over the last three years," he said. "I think maybe we were so much in love that it scared us. We were a lot younger then. Not only physically, but emotionally. I guess the thought of settling into some kind of permanent relationship, some happily ever after, didn't sit well with either one of us."

He paused, studying her a moment. She was nodding, vaguely, as if seeing that time through different eyes.

"But the thing is, Leese, I've always thought

it was a mistake. I should never have let you go. I just thought you wanted—"

"Let *me* go?" she said.

He nodded. "It seemed like what you wanted. So I made up that stupid story about California, to make it easier for you. To let you off the hook."

Her face opened up in surprise. "You're kidding, right?"

"No," he said. "Why would I be?"

She started laughing now, more tears springing to her eyes. She wiped them with her sleeve. "I don't believe this. And all this time I thought *you* were the one who wanted to break up."

Rafe frowned. "What?"

"I was letting *you* off the hook. I figured you didn't want to be tied down to someone."

Now Rafe started laughing, not quite believing what he was hearing.

"You don't know how miserable I was," Lisa said. "There were so many times I wanted to call you, tell you we'd made a mistake, especially after…" She paused, looking like a woman who had nearly dropped a toe on the trigger of a bear trap. "I just never got up the nerve, because I figured the last person you wanted to hear from was me."

"I felt exactly the same way," Rafe said. "How stupid are we?"

Now they both laughed, but there was a bittersweet quality to it. Then Rafe sobered, thinking about the little girl who lay upstairs, asleep by now. The little girl who had given him a pink kitty cat to keep the blue one company.

"And look what I missed because of it," he said.

"What do you mean?"

"This'll probably sound crazy to you, but when I look at your daughter, when I look at Chloe, all I can think is what might have been. She could be *my* daughter, not Sloan's. And instead of going through all this nonsense with him, you and I could have been making a home and raising our child."

Lisa's face went through a series of shifting emotions, as if she couldn't quite figure out how to respond. He'd taken a risk, telling her this, but it was the way he felt. And he'd been feeling it since he walked into her living room just a few short hours ago.

He had never been able to put her fully out of his mind, so it was no surprise that he was still in love with her.

Lisa again wiped the tears from her eyes

and said, "Rafe, I've been looking for a way to tell you this, so I guess it's best that I just come out and—"

She was cut off by the opening of the front door. Grandma Natalie stepped outside carrying a small tray, breaking the spell, jerking them back to reality.

"You two are looking quite cozy," she said.

Rafe smiled. "Just like old times."

Nonna glanced at Lisa as if they were in some sort of secret communication. "Am I interrupting something?" she asked.

That was odd, Rafe thought. Had they been talking about him? And, if so, why?

Then Lisa suddenly said, "No, no, Nonna. You're fine. We were just talking about the good old days…"

"You're sure, now?"

"I'm sure," Lisa said, and Rafe still wondered what the heck was going on between them.

Women and their talk.

But before he could give it too much thought, Grandma Natalie shuffled toward them with the tray, which held two cups of tea and a plate full of what she'd always called apostle's fingers. The dessert was made of ricotta cheese, sugar and cinnamon, and Rafe had been eating it for as long as he could remember.

"I prepared a treat for you," Nonna said. "I hope you aren't too full."

But Rafe was stuffed after dinner and took this as his cue to stand up. "As much as I don't want to, I'm gonna have to decline, Nonna. My shift starts in a couple hours and I need to get home to shower and shave."

"You're leaving? So soon?"

Rafe smiled. "Duty calls." He glanced at Lisa. "But don't worry, I'll be back."

He wanted to lean down and kiss her, especially after the conversation they'd just had. But agreeing that what they'd done in the past was a mistake didn't necessarily translate into how Lisa felt here and now. He sensed a hesitation in her, some kind of inner turmoil. But they'd have to finish their talk at another time. Hopefully soon.

So he merely nodded to her, said goodnight, then turned to take the steps down to his car. He was only halfway through the turn when Grandma Natalie took hold of his elbow.

"Wait, now, Rafael. Don't let an old woman chase you away. You two have so much to talk about."

"I'd like to stay, Nonna, but duty calls."

"Duty, duty, duty," she said. "That's all I ever heard from your grandfather. Why is everyone in this family so dedicated to duty?"

She was one to talk. In her early years she had been a probation officer for the state, and quite devoted to the job.

Rafe shrugged. "I guess we're all just wired that way."

"You can't just stay for a few more minutes? Maybe the young lady has something to—"

"That's okay, Nonna," Lisa said. "I'll still be here when he's off work. I should probably be getting ready for bed."

Rafe still sensed that something was going on here, something he wasn't privy to, but he merely nodded again, said another goodnight.

Then he took the steps down to the drive and got in his car.

AS THEY WATCHED him drive away, Grandma Natalie said, "Well, child? Did I just ruin your perfect moment?"

"I don't know if there is one, Nonna. Now probably wasn't the right time anyway."

"Oh, nonsense. The boy needs to know he

has blood. Every man does. It isn't fair to keep him in the dark any longer. That girl isn't getting any younger and every minute is precious. She needs a father. One who will love her and cherish her and take care of her."

"And do you think Rafe's that man?" Lisa asked.

Grandma Natalie scowled. "What kind of a silly question is that? You *know* he is."

Lisa nodded. She was right, of course. Having all these doubts about how Rafe would react to the news was nothing more than her own insecurities showing through. And as much as she'd wanted to tell him, she had almost welcomed the interruption from Grandma Natalie.

Why was she making this so complicated?

Maybe her problem was not that she was afraid Rafe would reject Chloe. Based on how they were interacting, based on what he had just told her, that seemed unlikely.

But they had spent the past few moments talking about what *could* have been, not what was. And while Rafe might not reject Chloe—would he reject *her?*

Was it too late for them to paint that perfect portrait of a happy family?

Her fear of the answer was, in itself, an

answer to the question she had asked herself earlier today.

Was she still in love with him?

Of course she was.

She had never *stopped* loving him.

Sitting here on this porch swing, talking about the silly mistake they had made—believing the other wanted to be set free—Lisa had felt that old chemistry ignite. For a moment she had thought Rafe was about to kiss her, but he had shied away from it.

The question was why?

Was it possible that he had indeed moved on?

Was it possible that he would never feel the way he'd felt back in college?

The way *she* felt *now?*

Was he merely caught up in the nostalgia of the moment, a feeling that would eventually fade, leaving nothing of substance in its wake?

As usual, she was overthinking. A habit she'd had since childhood.

But she couldn't help herself. Any more than she could help the knot in her stomach. The fear that what they'd once had could never again be duplicated.

Chapter Eighteen

The moment Rafe parked in the underground garage, he felt something wrong.

It wasn't a feeling he could quantify. More of an animal instinct, really. But it permeated the air around him as he climbed from the car.

Was someone watching him?

He thought about the look Oliver Sloan had given him outside the processing center. Sloan surrounded by a group of reporters, but locking eyes with Rafe, telling him, *Don't think you're gonna get away with this, hotshot.*

Could Sloan be stupid enough to have sent a couple goons to Rafe's apartment building?

Did he think that Rafe could be so easily intimidated?

If so, he was sadly mistaken. Rafe was long past the time in his life when someone like Sloan could scare him. And he'd already proven that Sloan's goons were ineffectual thugs who were all posture and no follow-through. Rafe's skills in Krav Maga had taken care of that, and they surely would again.

Not that Rafe felt he was anything special. But one thing his martial arts classes had taught him was that there was never a reason to feel helpless in the arms of danger. On the contrary, if you stayed smart and acted decisively, 99 percent of dangerous situations could be neutralized in a split second.

And if that last 1 percent required deadly force, then so be it. Rafe had never had any desire to kill a man, but he wouldn't hesitate to use that option if the situation required it.

He stood by his car and scanned the parking lot. His apartment building wasn't huge, and the lot itself was small, full of narrow spaces packed with a couple dozen cars. Entry required a key card, which took you past a rolling steel gate, but such safeguards could be easily hacked by savvy people, either through electronics or simple social engineering.

But as he searched the dimly lit, cement enclosure, paying special attention to the dark pockets behind the parked cars, he saw nothing of concern. No movement. No subtle shifting of shadows.

Yet that feeling of being watched didn't fade. If someone *was* watching him, he was very, very good.

Locking up the Mustang, Rafe went to his trunk and retrieved his uniform, holster and Glock. Bundling up the uniform and holster, he tucked them under his arm and kept the Glock in his hand, just in case.

With another quick glance around him, he crossed from his car to the elevator about ten yards away, feeling the hairs on the back of neck rise as he pressed the button and waited.

He half expected someone to come up behind him, but the elevator arrived without incident, its doors sliding open at the sound of a bell.

HALF A MINUTE LATER, Rafe stepped into the tenth-floor hallway, which was dotted with several doors. His apartment was on the far side of the hall, and he moved toward it, only to stop short about three yards away.

His door was ajar.

Rafe tensed, chucked his uniform to the hallway floor. Raising the Glock, he studied the open door for a long moment, then stepped carefully toward it, coming in at an angle, approaching it from the side.

He stopped again, just shy of the door. Gave it a nudge with the toe of his right boot.

The door creaked. Swung open just wide enough to fit through. Dark inside.

Rafe waited. Listened.

Heard nothing.

Yet he sensed that someone was in there, the hairs on the back of his neck still tingling, those animal instincts again kicking in.

He waited a moment longer, then decided to move. Inching laterally toward the opening, he nudged it wider, then quickly slipped through, immediately stepping to the side to stay out of the light from the hallway.

Pressing his back against the wall, he gripped the Glock with both hands, waited again. He listened for the sound of breathing.

Nothing.

He reached for the light switch next to him, flipped it on. The lamps on either side of his couch came to life, illuminating the small apartment, and he was surprised by what he saw.

The place was mess. A disaster. All the books had been pulled from the bookshelves. The drawers and cabinets in his kitchenette hung open, several utensils scattered across the floor. The door to his bedroom hung wide and in the wan light he could see that his mattress had been overturned, the comforter and bedsheets lying in a heap on the floor.

His apartment had been ransacked.

But by whom? And what were they looking for?

These questions had only just entered his mind, when he heard a faint *click* and a lamp went on his bedroom.

Rafe crouched, raised the Glock, then froze.

His sister, Kate, was sitting in the armchair he kept in the corner near the bed.

What the heck?

"Nice entry, little brother. But I had you for two or three milliseconds when you stepped into the doorway. You should've killed the hallway light first."

Rafe stood up, his heart pounding. "What is this?" he barked. "What are you doing here?"

Kate gestured. "You want to put the weapon away?"

He'd almost forgotten he was pointing it at her. He lowered it, tucked it into his waistband and said, "That doesn't answer my question."

Kate got to her feet and approached him.

He noticed now that she was holding a manila folder with a department tab on the side. A case file.

"Why don't we start with your answering a couple of mine?"

Rafe frowned. "What's going on here?" He gestured to the mess. "Did you do this?"

She shook her head. "But I know who did."

"Who? Sloan?"

She shook her head again and waggled a hand toward his small two-seater dining table. "Let's talk, all right?"

Moving to the table, she dropped the manila folder on top of it and sat, waiting for him to join her. He crossed to it, scraped the second chair back and sank onto it, feeling the Glock pinch at him. He pulled it free and laid it on the table.

"Okay," he said. "Start talking."

Kate nodded. "I have to say, little brother, I'm disappointed in you."

"About what?"

She stared at him a long moment.

"Well?" he said.

She drummed her fingers on the folder. "You mind telling me where you were at around 3:30 today?"

Rafe felt his gut tighten. All at once he knew what this was about.

He'd been made.

He didn't know how, but Kate wouldn't be here if she didn't suspect, or know for certain, that he'd been at Azarov's apartment this afternoon. That *he* was the one she'd been chasing.

"I guess I don't need to tell you that," he said. "Because you already know."

Her fingers went still and she slid the manila folder across to him. Rafe stared down at it, saw that the label read CASE 13-2257. HOMICIDE.

He flipped it open and found a photograph inside. One taken by a traffic cam as a car passed through the red at an intersection.

The car that had nearly hit him.

Rafe hadn't even noticed the flash of the cam, but there he stood in living color, dodging that car, his face presented directly to the camera. Identification wasn't iffy, it was crystal clear. The guy in the hoodie was, without a doubt, Rafael Franco.

"You care to explain?" Kate said.

Rafe lowered his head, could barely look at her. Kate had always had this uncanny ability to make him feel small. In her presence he was the screwed-up younger brother who couldn't get anything right.

It was an unfair characterization, sure. But he felt it, nevertheless. Even though he knew she loved him fiercely and with all her heart.

What he always saw in her eyes at times like this was disappointment.

He finally looked at her again. "I was trying to get a lead on the killings," he said. "I know I was out of line, but I was hoping to find a connection to Oliver Sloan."

"Because of the ex-wife? Lisa?"

He nodded. "I need that guy put away. I don't want him going near her again."

"Sounds like you're letting a certain part of your body do your thinking for you."

"Yeah," Rafe said. "My heart. I'm still in love with her, Kate. And I don't want that creep terrorizing her."

"Are you sure that's all it is?"

He furrowed his brow at her. "What do you mean?"

She gestured to the folder in front of him. "Look at the next page."

Rafe moved the photo aside and stared down at a department ballistics report. He quickly read through it, saw that the techs had found a match between the bullets found in the bodies of the Russians to a SIG Sauer that had been recovered in a search.

"You found the murder weapon?"

"Yes, we did."

"Where?"

Kate was again silent for a long moment. Then she said, "I think you already know the answer to that."

Rafe was at a loss. "I do?"

Kate nodded and hooked thumb toward his bedroom doorway. "They found it under your mattress, Rafe. Pretty stupid place to hide it."

Intense heat rushed to Rafe's face and his stood up, feeling his heart start to pound all over again. *"What?"*

"Sit down, Rafe."

"I don't know what it is you're accusing me—"

"Sit *down,* Rafe."

Big sis again.

He took a breath, sat back down, waited for Kate to explain.

"I've known you all your life, little brother. You were never a stupid kid, and you're certainly not a stupid man. Your work in the field, until now, has been exemplary, and I'm pretty sure you were on the fast track to Homicide. I don't know that for sure, but there was talk about it." She paused, reached across the table and tapped the ballistics report. "But this doesn't look good, Rafe. As soon as Eberhart saw the photo and we realized who we were chasing this afternoon, he went straight to Internal Affairs."

"What?"

"I tried to talk him out of it, begged him to give me a chance to speak to you first. But you know Charlie. Always by the book, and he never has liked you."

"No kidding," Rafe said.

"Internal Affairs tossed the apartment, found the gun, then rushed through the ballistics report."

"This is complete nonsense," Rafe said. "That gun isn't mine."

"Maybe so, but as I said, they found it under your mattress. And that isn't all they found."

Rafe furrowed his brow again. "I'm listening."

She took hold of the ballistics report and flipped it aside. Beneath it was a printout of some bank records, the name RAFAEL FRANCO and his account number referenced at the top of the sheet.

Kate tapped one of the entries. "There's a

new deposit this morning. You want to tell me where you got that kind of money?"

Rafe zeroed in on the entry. It read $10,000.

He swallowed hard, his heart pounding again, not quite believing what he saw.

Where the heck had this money come…?

Then it hit him. Sloan. Oliver Sloan. The creep wasn't coming at him with his ineffectual goons. No, that was too obvious, and likely to get Sloan in trouble.

This was a frame job, pure and simple. Sloan was framing him for the hit on the Russians.

Don't think you're gonna get away with this, hotshot.

"I'm being set up," he said.

"Believe me, I tried to tell them that, but the boys in Internal Affairs aren't buying it. They think you were paid to do the hit and were probably in Azarov's apartment trying to plant evidence, pin it on Sloan."

"You've gotta be kidding me. So, what… is IA in Sloan's pocket, too?"

Kate shook her head. "They have to go where the evidence leads, Rafe. You know that. We all do. And right now it points to you."

Rafe closed his eyes. "I can't believe this is happening."

"It took everything I had to convince them to let me talk to you first. That's why I'm here."

"You know I didn't do this, right?"

Kate nodded. "I know you'd never hurt anyone. Not like this. Not unless it was necessary force. You were raised under the code, just as I was."

He studied her eyes and knew she was being sincere. Not that he'd ever doubt her.

"So what happens next?" he asked.

"You know the drill. You'll be booked and interrogated, unless you lawyer up. And I'd advise you to lawyer up."

"I can't say anything incriminating if I don't know anything."

Kate sighed. "Come on, Rafael, I know Ma didn't raise an idiot. I'll make some calls, get an attorney for you."

"And then what?"

"What else? We fight this thing."

"We?"

"You may be a bonehead, little brother, but you're my blood. And blood is everything."

She gathered up the photograph and ballistics report, returned them to the file, then closed it and stood up.

"Are you handling the arrest?" Rafe asked.

"Nope."

"IA?"

She nodded, then took her cell phone from her pocket, dialed a number and murmured a few words into it.

As they waited for IA to arrive, Kate said, "By the way, you almost gave me heart attack this afternoon with that little running stunt. It took me ten minutes just to catch my breath."

"Sorry about that."

"Just do me favor," she said. "Next time I yell at you to stop, do what I say, okay?"

Chapter Nineteen

The boys in Internal Affairs were a humorless bunch. But then Rafe figured it was hard to have a sense of humor when 90 percent of the department despised you.

They put him in an interrogation room and fired questions at him, using the usual IA bulldog approach, trying to intimidate him, wanting to know who had ordered the hit and why. But Rafe took Kate's advice and immediately lawyered up.

In his experience, a perp who called in an attorney right away only made himself look more guilty to the people investigating him. But at this point, Rafe didn't care what they thought. If he started flapping his mouth, they might misconstrue something he said as evidence of his involvement in the crime, or even an outright confession.

Most of the people they brought into these rooms were indeed guilty of what they'd been accused of. But Rafe was one of the exceptions, and much to their frustration, he wasn't about to give them ammunition against him.

The lawyer was there within an hour of his confinement. A small, compact, athletic guy with short-cropped hair and an expensive suit. And Rafe wondered if he'd be able to *afford* the guy.

But then he was $10,000 richer, wasn't he? Sloan had made sure of that.

The next hour was spent being hammered by another round of twenty questions, only this time the lawyer, whose name was Chaplin, shut the investigators down at every opportunity.

They didn't like him much.

When they realized they were getting nowhere, they hauled Rafe off to a holding cell and let him sit there the rest of the night.

And all he could think about, as he stared at those cement walls, was finding a way to make bail, clear his name—and, most important, protect Lisa and her little girl.

Whatever it took.

HE WAS ARRAIGNED the next morning at 9:00 a.m., sharing the perp bench with an accused car thief and an armed robber. It was ironic to be sitting here in the very same court that Sloan had sat in yesterday—only Rafe, even with his cop family, didn't have the kind of connections that would spring him.

He was charged with two counts of first-degree homicide and gave the judge a loud and forceful "Not guilty" when asked how he wanted to plea.

Arraignments are by and large a formality in which every defendant pleads not guilty. It's rare for an arraignment judge to allow any other plea, for fear the defendant hasn't had a chance to consult with an attorney. Better to take a "not guilty" and accept a modified plea later, should the state and the defendant reach an agreement before trial.

It had always annoyed Rafe when the news media went into a frenzy of outrage over a high-profile defendant who had declared himself not guilty. If they were honest in their reporting, they'd tell their audience that this was standard practice in any criminal court.

Once Rafe pled, the judge said, "As to the matter of bail, what's the state's recommendation?"

The prosecutor, a fat man in a thin man's suit, cleared his throat. "This is a heinous crime, your honor. Two men shot dead in cold blood. So we ask that the defendant be held without bail."

Not what Rafe wanted to hear, but he wasn't surprised.

"You're honor," his attorney said. "My client is a well-regarded member of the law enforcement community. He has no prior record, no means for flight and is in no way responsible for these two deaths. We'd ask that he be released on his own recognizance."

"You can set that pipe dream aside," the judge told him, "but I'm not going with the prosecution's recommendation, either. Bail is set at $2 million."

"But, your honor," Chaplin cried, "that's as good as setting no bail at all. My client doesn't have the means for that kind of bond."

The judge pounded his gavel. "Not my problem, counsel. Next case."

As they moved aside to let the next attorney and his client step up to the bench, Chaplin said, "Not the outcome I was hoping for, but don't sweat it. You'll be out in about two hours."

"How?" Rafe said. "I don't have that kind of money. And neither does my family."

"But you do have an angel on your side."

Rafe studied him. "Angel? What are you talking about?"

The attorney hooked his thumb to the gallery behind them and Rafe turned, surprised to see Lisa sitting in the back row.

Had she been here all this time?

She was watching Rafe with concern in her eyes. Gave him a small wave.

He waved back, then turned to Chaplin. "Are you saying she's putting up on the bond?"

"Putting up her *house,* as a matter of fact. Which is kind of ironic, since it was paid for by Sloan."

"I can't let her do that."

"What are you, nuts?" Chaplin said. "It'll be at least two months before your trial starts. You want to be sitting in a cement room all that time?"

"But it's her *house,*" Rafe said.

"Relax, Franco, it's just collateral. She doesn't lose anything as long as you show up for your court dates. And you don't strike me as the kind of guy who would skip out on court."

"Why's that?"

Chaplin smirked. "You've got a family full of cops. Where you going to hide?"

"YOU REALLY SHOULDN'T have done this," Rafe said.

They were sitting in back of a cab, headed toward Rafe's apartment. He noted that Lisa was wearing a gray jacket for the occasion, one he had given her for her twenty-first birthday. It was a bit dated, fashionwise, and he was not only surprised she had worn it, but that she'd kept it at all.

Rafe had always loved the way the jacket fit her. A gentle caressing of her curves. He was suddenly reminded of the night she he had worn it—and nothing else—as she crawled atop him in bed and made him forget all about a looming trig exam. Made him forget about everything except her, wearing that simple swatch of tailored gray cloth over that magnificent—and pliant—body.

Was wearing it now a signal of some kind? Was she trying to tell him something? Was it a symbol of solidarity, love, or simply just a jacket?

"I had to do it, Rafe," she said. "I know this all happened because of me."

"Don't be ridiculous."

"I know this has to be Oliver's doing. He's done it out of spite and jealousy, and if he's as powerful as you say he is, he'd be able to call on the right people to make it happen."

Rafe had, of course, been thinking the exact same thing, but Lisa hadn't provoked Sloan. *He* had.

"You weren't the one who stormed into your ex's hotel suite and arrested him," he said. "You weren't the one who broke into a victim's apartment and ran from his own sister. Believe me, this is my own stupidity at work. But I was looking for a way to get Sloan out of your life without..."

He didn't finish the sentence.

"Without what?" she asked.

Rafe hesitated, wondering how much he should tell her. But he knew he needed to be open and honest with her. He'd learned that the hard way.

"My bosses called me into a meeting yesterday. After Sloan was freed. They've been investigating him for months."

"If he's what you say he is, then that's a good thing, isn't it?"

"Yes," he said. "But they had a proposition for me. One they tried to make very difficult to refuse."

She frowned. "What kind of proposition?"

"They wanted me to turn you."

"Turn me?"

"They wanted me to use my influence with you, to use our past, to try to get on your good side and convince you to cooperate."

She stiffened. "Cooperate in what way?"

"They wanted me to convince you to encourage Sloan to return to you so that you could spy on him and report back to me."

Her eyes hardened. "And did you agree to this?"

"No."

She didn't seem to have heard his response. "So is that what this has all been about? Taking us to Nonna's house? Being so nice to Chloe?"

"No," Rafe said forcefully. "Of course not. I would never do that to you. I would never do anything to put you or Chloe in danger. That's why I broke into that apartment. I was hoping to find something that would connect the guy's murder to Sloan."

She softened, considered this a moment. Then tears sprang to her eyes as she said, "So then this did happen because of me. I've made your life a mess."

He grabbed hold of her hand. "Stop that, Leese. *You* didn't do anything. This is all on me."

They let that hang in the air for a moment, then she laced her fingers through his and squeezed. "You don't know how much I've missed you, Rafe. How many times I've cursed myself for letting you go."

"You don't think I feel the same way?"

Her eyes looked hopeful. "Do you?"

He looked into them, tears and all, thinking what a waste these past three years had been without her. Thinking how a simple miscommunication between them had separated them for far too long. And of the irony that it was fate—and Oliver Sloan—that had brought them back together.

On the porch last night, he had hesitated. But not now. He leaned toward her, kissed her. Felt the heat of her breath, her desire.

And there were no mistakes this time.

They both knew exactly what the other wanted.

Chapter Twenty

They made love in the shower.

When they first entered Rafe's apartment, Lisa was shocked by the mess, once again feeling guilty that this had all happened because of her. Despite Rafe's insistence that he was the one at fault, she knew that he would never have gotten into this trouble if he hadn't been trying to protect her.

She took one look at the open cupboards and drawers and the books and papers strewn across the floor and immediately pushed him toward the bedroom.

"Go get yourself cleaned up," she said. "You smell like the inside of a jail cell."

He had laughed, kissed her on the nose, then headed toward his bathroom.

When he was gone, Lisa got to work. The least she could do to thank him was clean the place up.

She started with the kitchenette, making sure the dishes, canned goods and paper products were all back in place, that drawers were all shut, then she moved on to the living room and started returning the books to their shelves.

She was halfway through the pile, listening to the sound of Rafe's shower, when she found a book that momentarily stopped her heart. It was a copy of Robert Frost's poems that she had given to him shortly before they'd split up.

There was a bookmark poking up from the pages and Lisa cracked the book open to it, finding a small strip of photo booth snapshots. Four photographs of her and Rafe mugging for the camera, taken at a shopping mall one day when they had ditched their classes.

Lisa remembered that day well, especially what they'd done that afternoon on Rafe's bed. The almost insatiable desire they'd shared.

In the book itself, there was a highlighted sentence, Frost's words staring up to her, speaking to her, as if the poet—and Rafe— had read her mind:

Love is an irresistible desire to be irresistibly desired.

A moment later, the books and the mess

were forgotten and Lisa was in Rafe's bathroom, pulling off her clothes, looking in through the steamed glass at his newly toned body, as the water cascaded over his broad shoulders, the expanse of his chest, dusted lightly with hair, the trail that hair made downward past the ripple of his abs and below.

She stared openly at him, feeling the desire overwhelm her, moisten her, as she opened the shower door and stepped into his arms. She offered herself to him, pressing her nipples against his chest, feeling the brush of his firmness against her thigh. Feeling it grow and expand as if begging to be touched.

So she obliged, reaching a hand down to squeeze, remembering the feel of him as if it were only yesterday, yet experiencing it in a whole new way, now that he had grown from a boy into very much a man.

They immediately fell into their old rhythm, Lisa now dropping to her knees, feeling the warmth of the water rushing over her shoulders as she took him into her mouth.

She heard him groan and the sound empowered her, thrilled her, knowing that she was giving him the ultimate pleasure. He put his hands on her head, and she felt them tighten against her as she worked. She knew instinctively that it had been a long time since he'd experienced this. Knew instinctively that he was coming close.

She felt his hands tugging at her, trying to get her to stand up so that they could move on to even better things, but she stayed put, wanting to reward him quickly for his sacrifices, to thank him for being there for her. It wouldn't have to stop here, of course. She already knew that they'd be moving into the bedroom after this, throwing that mattress back on its bedframe and continuing where they left off.

So she ignored him and concentrated on her task, feeling him grow even harder, listening to his groans, his breaths become more rapid.

Then he stiffened, his fingers wrapped up in her hair, tightening against her head as he let out a final, tortured moan and released himself.

She held him there until he was done, then gently pulled away and got to her feet, falling into his arms again, holding him close as she waited for the wave to roll over him and dissipate.

And, as she predicted, they didn't stop there.

THEY DIDN'T BOTHER to dry off, didn't bother to put the mattress on the bedframe. They simply knocked it flat on the floor and fell on top of it, their drenched skin soaking the bedsheets.

But neither one cared.

Rafe's hands began to roam, finding her breasts, gripping her enflamed nipples between his fingers, a tingle of electricity shooting through Lisa as his mouth found hers, his tongue slipping urgently between her lips.

Then one of his hands slid down her belly, stopping for a moment to caress her navel, sending a jolt straight to the sweet spot. She moaned in his ear as he moved on, using those strong fingers, caressing her, pressing the heel of his palm against her pelvis as he explored.

More shutters of electricity shot through her, tunneling straight for her brain, tiny explosions of pleasure bursting like the *rat-tat-tat* of a machine gun, growing in intensity as his fingers continued to move, to caress, to press and pinch and pull.

Then he pulled his hand away and slid down her body, tattooing her with kisses along the way, moving his mouth to her pelvis, using his tongue in place of his fingers, the tiny explosions growing in intensity.

She suddenly realized that her legs were trembling uncontrollably, something that had never happened to her before, even with Rafe. She was almost embarrassed by her inability to control them, but decided to go with the moment, let her body react however it chose to.

This feeling was too exquisite to fight.

She knew Rafe was merely reciprocating for what she'd done to him in the shower, but she had forgotten how skilled he was at this, and the reminder was so raw and real that she could barely contain herself.

Even so, she wanted him inside her. It had only been a few minutes since they left the shower, but she was more than ready for him and hoped that he was up to the task.

He must have read her mind, because he stopped suddenly and got up on his knees before her. And she shouldn't have wondered about him, because there, below the ripple of his abs, he was ready to go again.

And he looked enormous. Bigger than in the shower.

Bigger than she remembered from their days together.

He put a hand on each of her knees and gently pushed her legs apart, lowering himself toward her, rubbing against her as if priming her for what was to come.

But she didn't need priming. She was more than ready. Was, in fact, desperate for him. She needed him inside her.

Now.

A split second later she got her wish as he thrust hard and deep, filling her completely, his heat radiating up through her, growing in intensity with each new thrust.

She heard someone moaning, and realized it was her. A loud, long, uncontrolled utterance, punctuated by those thrusts.

And now Rafe was moaning again, too, the sound filling her ears, heightening her excitement. She felt the current between them growing stronger, hotter, more electric, building and building, their breaths shortening, timed perfectly to the rhythm of their bodies.

Then, all at once, something gave way inside her, something charged and fluid that worked its way toward her brain and blossomed there.

She squeezed her eyes shut and let go, drifting away on a wave of pleasure, letting it crash over her.

Then Rafe uttered a low moan and tensed, and she felt him throbbing inside her, releasing himself, his warm wetness filling her, feeding her, pleasing her.

Then he collapsed against her and brought his mouth to hers, his breath hot and earthy, as he said softly, "I...love...you..."

And despite everything wonderful about the passion that had consumed her—had consumed them both—those three words were the real magic. And the only thing that mattered to her.

LATER, AS THEY LAY curled in each other's arms, Lisa said, "I've been thinking about what you told me."

He smiled, nuzzled her neck. "Just now? That I love you?"

"Well...yes, but no."

He got up his elbow. "Because I do, you know. That wasn't just a heat-of-the-moment thing. I've never stopped loving you, Leese. I don't think it's humanly possible."

She smiled and pressed her nose against his chin. "I feel the same way, Rafe, but that's not what I mean."

"Then what?"

"I'm talking about what you told me in the cab. About your bosses wanting you to turn me."

"Forget that. I didn't even entertain the notion for a second."

"I know," she said, "but maybe you should have."

He froze, narrowed his eyes at her. "What are you talking about?"

It was a thought she'd harbored since the moment he told her.

"Maybe I should do what they want," she said. "Maybe I should go undercover, so to speak, make Oliver think he still has a chance with me. Try to help their investi—"

"Forget it. That's not going to happen."

"But what if I can find some way to—"

He sat upright. "I said forget it. There's no way I'm letting them put you in that kind of danger. If he were to find out what you were up to, I have no doubt he'd have you killed. You'd wind up just like Azarov and his partner, sitting in a Jaguar with a bullet in your head."

He was heated now. Obviously troubled by the mere notion of her doing something like this. So she backed down, didn't press it.

"All right," she said. "You're right."

"You better believe I am."

"It was just a thought. I want to help in some way. I want to…"

She paused as the name he had spoken finally resonated.

Azarov.

"My God," she said.

"What's wrong?"

"That name. Azarov. I've heard it before. Well, not really heard it, but I've seen it on a document."

He nodded. "He would've been listed on the prosecutor's complaint against me as one of the victims."

Lisa shook her head. "No, no. Not today. A long time ago. Over a year now."

"What are you talking about? Where?"

Lisa took a breath, thinking about what she'd done in hopes that it would keep Oliver from contesting the divorce and ensure that he'd back away from her. She had always thought what she had found had something to do with a shady real estate deal, but now she wondered if it was much more than that.

"When I asked Oliver for a divorce," she said, "he outright refused. Said there was nothing I could ever do that would persuade him to let me go."

"Yet he did."

She nodded. "Because I managed to get some leverage against him. I knew he was involved in some unsavory real estate deals, so I searched his home computer and found a password-protected folder containing documents that I thought were connected to one of them. Names, dates, addresses, amounts. It looked like an accounting of bribes that had been paid out to various recipients."

"How did you know the password?"

"Oliver's pretty easy to read. I just kept guessing until I got it right."

"And that's where you saw Azarov's name?"

"Yes," she said. "It didn't click when you first said it, but now I'm sure of it. And I'm wondering if what I saw wasn't evidence of a real estate scam at all. Maybe those documents prove that Oliver has ties to organized crime."

Rafe's eyes were alive now. "Tell me you made a copy."

She nodded again. "On a data chip. I hid it in a safe place, and gave Oliver an ultimatum. Divorce me or I turn it over to the police. I had no idea if it would pay off, but judging by the look on his face, it was something pretty damaging. And it was enough to make him leave me alone." She paused. "For a while, at least."

"I'm surprised he left you alone as long as he did. He's a creature of impulse."

"No kidding," she said. "Ninety percent of it fueled by testosterone."

"So where did you hide this data chip?"

She sat up now and kissed his cheek. "Get dressed."

Chapter Twenty-One

They were halfway across town when Rafe realized they were being followed.

Three cars back. A gray BMW sedan that should have blended in with the rest of the traffic, but didn't.

Rafe had noticed it shortly after they left his parking garage, but hadn't given it much thought until the car made a couple of tricky maneuvers to keep pace with the Mustang.

So there was no question about it. There was somebody unfriendly back there.

There were two possibilities. Either it was IA, trying to keep tabs on their number-one suspect, or it was one of Sloan's goons, keeping tabs on Lisa.

Either way, the news wasn't good.

"This is going to sound like the biggest cliché in the world," he said, "but we've got company."

"What do you mean?" She started to turn

her head to look behind them but Rafe quickly put a hand on her wrist, stopping her.

"Hold it," he said. "No point in letting them know we know about them."

Lisa looked worried. "Who do you think it is?"

"I've got a couple of guesses, but figure it could go either way." He sighed. "No matter who it is, they don't need to know where we're headed and what we're up to. Not yet, at least."

"So then what's the plan?"

"You remember that roller-coaster ride we went on at Hampton Park our junior year?"

She made a face. "How could I forget? I threw up all over your car. Why?"

"Don't do it again," he said, then stomped on the accelerator.

The Mustang roared and shot forward through an intersection. Rafe spun the wheel, took a sharp right, then shifted, stomped again and shot into the left lane as he poured on the gas.

Checking his rearview mirror, he saw the Beemer take the turn behind him, coming toward them at a clip. If the driver had been trying to hide earlier, there was no such subterfuge now. The driver came after them like a sleek gray cheetah, obviously unconcerned about rising gas prices.

Rafe had seen his share of high-speed chases in the past couple years, but he'd never been on the receiving end of one of them. Cutting off a Chevy Malibu, he changed lanes and picked up speed. The switch was abrupt and jerky, Lisa's face going pale as she grabbed for the handbar above her door.

"Uh…uh…uh…" she said, her widening eyes on the road ahead, apparently unable to form any words.

"Hang on!" Rafe told her, then shot past another car, cut back into the left lane and made an arcing turn onto an adjoining street. The Mustang's tires screamed in protest as they burned up the road.

Checking the rearview mirror again, Rafe saw the BMW breeze through the turn with a smooth, steady hand.

This guy was good.

Rafe checked his speedometer. He was clocking a good seventy miles an hour on a city street and his pursuer wasn't even flinching. No way the guy was IA.

Not with those skills.

And Rafe doubted he was one of Sloan's usual thugs, either. The people Sloan surrounded himself with weren't exactly top-of-the-line.

So who was he?

Rafe decided there was only one way to find out. A face-to-face with the man. But not on *his* terms. It was time to reverse the trajectory of this chase and set it right.

Telling Lisa to hold on again, Rafe spun the wheel, tapped the brakes and roared into an alleyway on his right. He was familiar with this alley because of his patrol work and knew it led to an adjacent street.

On that street was another alleyway, this one long and narrow. But Rafe knew about an abandoned warehouse at about the half-way mark, and a service ramp that led into an empty cargo bay.

Sheriff's deputies routinely patrolled the alleyway to chase away squatters, and after a concerted six-month effort the vagrants had finally gotten the message and stayed away for good. The owner was supposed to have boarded the place up by now, but hadn't yet gotten around to it.

When Rafe saw the gray Beemer turn into the alley behind him, he stomped on the gas again and shot out into the street. Horns honked around him as he cut diagonally toward the second alleyway and turned into it, shooting straight for that warehouse ramp.

A few moments later, he pulled into the darkness of a cargo bay, then came to a stop and let the engine idle.

Lisa seemed to be trying to find her voice. "...You were right about the roller coaster."

"Sorry about that."

"What are we doing in here?"

"Waiting."

"For what?"

"The inevitable," Rafe said cryptically, feeling a little guilty for not explaining his plan. "I need you to get out of the car."

"What?"

"This could get nasty, and I don't want you getting hurt. You'll be safe enough here in the warehouse."

"But I don't understand. Where are you—"

Rafe put a finger to his lips to silence her as the sound of the BMW's engine reverberated through the alleyway. Getting the message, she carefully popped her door open and got out of the car. She looked frightened, but it couldn't be helped. Better she hide in here in case this guy had firepower.

Nodding to her, Rafe watched her back away into the warehouse darkness, then popped the Mustang into Reverse and looked out the rear windshield toward the bottom of the ramp.

A moment later, the BMW rolled into view, cruising at a slow crawl now, the driver undoubtedly wary as he searched for his prey.

Rafe hit the gas. Hard.

He rocketed backward down the ramp, ramming into the side of the BMW. Metal screamed as it collapsed inward and the Beemer was punched sideways. Before the driver knew what hit him, Rafe cut the engine and was out of the car in a quick, fluid move, the spare gun he kept in his glove compartment now in hand as he turned toward the crumpled BMW.

But to his utter surprise, the driver was gone, his door hanging wide. How he had managed to flee so fast was beyond Rafe's comprehension, but Rafe spun on his heels, looked down the alley and saw a man running, wearing a hooded sweatshirt—much like the one Rafe had worn earlier—much like the one he'd seen the hit man wearing at the auto repair shop two nights ago.

And Rafe knew this was the same guy.

It had to be.

He shouted and took off after him, and the

guy turned suddenly, gun in hand, and fired off a shot.

The bullet whizzed past Rafe as he dove behind a garbage bin and returned fire, once, twice, but the guy was too far away now, heading into the street.

And then something completely unexpected happened.

Just as Rafe was about to get to his feet and give chase again, just as the guy had stepped onto the street—

An A-1 Furniture truck came out of nowhere and slammed into the man, killing him instantly.

Rafe stopped short and turned away, squeezing his eyes shut in horror.

"No ID," Kate said. "Nothing. This guy's a phantom."

"I'd bet my last nickel he was working for Oliver Sloan," Rafe told her. "He's got to be a hired killer. I'm almost positive he's the guy I chased out of that auto repair shop."

They were standing in the mouth of the alley, a section of the street cordoned off as crime scene techs worked to bag the man's body and remove it.

Lisa stood nearby, looking pale and sickly,

undoubtedly trying her best not to throw up. Kate's partner, Eberhart, was leaning against their cruiser, quietly smoking a cigarette as he eyed Rafe suspiciously.

Kate frowned at Rafe. "What do you think you're doing, little brother?"

"What do you mean?"

"It looks to me as if you're still trying to work this case. And now you've gotten the ex-wife involved."

"You're the ones who wanted her involved, remember?"

"That was before IA arrested you. If you had any sense, you'd be lying very low right now. You need to stay away from this. As it is, my partner wants to haul you in right now and start grilling you."

"Hey," Rafe said. "I didn't ask for this guy to come after us. What happened here was purely defensive."

"Well, I guarantee IA'll have plenty of questions, but right now, you need to go home, get some rest, catch up with your girlfriend— who looks scared witless, by the way—and try to forget that Oliver Sloan even exists."

"Can't do that," Rafe said.

Kate sighed. "Look, I'm not telling you this as your big sister. I'm telling you this as a fellow cop. We're going to stop this guy, I promise you that, but it's going to take time to get the goods on him."

"Maybe not," Rafe said.

She studied him. "What do you mean?"

He gestured toward Lisa. "Turns out she may have some evidence that proves Sloan's not only connected to organized crime, but also to one of the victims, as well. Azarov."

"What kind of evidence?"

"Some documents Sloan kept hidden on his computer with names, dates and what she thinks may have been bribe amounts."

Kate looked visibly excited. "You've got to be kidding me. Where are these documents?"

"On a data chip she's been keeping in a safety deposit box. We were on our way to retrieve it when the dead man started following us."

"You sure this is the real thing?"

Rafe glanced at Lisa, their eyes connecting for a moment, then returned his gaze to Kate. "She wouldn't lie to me."

Kate didn't need any more prompting. She immediately turned, calling out to Eberhart. "Rev her up, Charlie, we've got places to go."

Eberhart frowned, ditched his cigarette. "Oh, yeah? Where to?"

"We're going to make a withdrawal."

THE HAMPTON BRANCH of the Westland National Bank was located in a strip mall in southwest St. Louis.

Rafe's Mustang had to be towed from the alley, so he and Lisa rode in the back of Kate's cruiser to their destination, which was little more than an oversize box, sandwiched between a Taco Hut and a Gino's Pizza.

As they all climbed out of the car, Eberhart said, "So this is where we find the evidence to take Sloan down, huh? Fat chance."

Kate said, "Why don't you wait out here, Charlie?"

"And miss the look on your face when this turns out to be a big fat bust?"

"Smoke another cigarette," she said. "I think you might need it."

Eberhart shrugged. "Suit yourself."

As he pulled his pack from his coat pocket and turned back to the car, Kate, Rafe and Lisa moved toward the bank's entrance. Rafe opened the door, letting Lisa and Kate step past him.

The bank was small, nothing more than a satellite office for one of the large branches downtown. Which, Lisa had told them, was exactly why she had chosen it.

There were two teller windows and a manager's desk off to the right. Toward the back was a cage with the vault on the left, and a small room full of safety deposit boxes on the right. The safety deposit clerk sat at a desk nearby, and looked up with a smile as they approached.

Lisa introduced herself and gave the clerk her account number. The clerk checked her records, nodded, looked at Lisa's photo ID then stood and escorted them past the gate into the security box room.

The clerk and Lisa approached a small door in the wall marked 339, and used dual keys in the locks to open it. The clerk slid the box out and handed it to Lisa, then excused herself, telling her that she could have privacy in a small, curtained booth to the left of the room.

When she was gone, they all moved to the booth. Lisa slid the curtain back and set the box on a table inside. As Rafe and Kate watched, she took hold of the lid and lifted it, Rafe feeling giddy with anticipation.

But disappointment soon followed.

The box was empty.

Her face filling with shock, Lisa shoved a hand inside and patted it—an instinctive, but ultimately useless gesture.

"I don't understand," she said. "I put it in here. I *know* I put it in here."

Kate glanced at Rafe as if to say, *Are you sure this woman's trustworthy?* But Rafe ignored her and grabbed hold of the box, turning it upside and shaking it.

Nothing fell out.

The data chip was clearly gone.

"Somebody must have taken it," Lisa said. "I don't know how they managed it, but—"

"We can certainly try to find out," Kate said, then turned and headed back toward the safety deposit clerk's desk.

They followed as Kate pulled out her badge and showed it to the clerk. "Excuse me, but I need you to check the records."

"For what?" the clerk asked.

"I want to know if anyone had access to that safety deposit box in the last several days."

"I'm afraid you'd need a warrant for that."

Lisa moved forward. "Are you forgetting that it's *my* box? Please do as she asks."

The clerk nodded, then jabbed a few keys on her computer keyboard, watching the screen. When she found what she needed, she said, "The records show that you came in three days ago to access the box."

Lisa frowned at her. "Oh, really? And do you remember seeing me?"

"I wasn't on duty that day. But it says here the customer complained of a lost key, so we used a master."

"You *what?*"

"It's all right here," the clerk said. "She had several forms of identification and there was no reason to believe—"

"This is ridiculous." Lisa shook her head in dismay, then staggered to a nearby chair and sat down.

Rafe and Kate moved to her.

"I can't believe it," she said. "I don't know how he found out where I was hiding it, but this has to be Oliver's doing. He must've found someone to pretend to be me."

"I wouldn't put it past him," Kate said.

Rafe nodded. "Which would explain why he suddenly showed up at your house the other night. You don't have any leverage against him. Not anymore."

Tears sprang to Lisa's eyes. "I can't believe this. Why won't he just leave me alone?"

"Because he's a psychopath," Rafe said. "He's fixated on you."

Lisa wiped her eyes. Rafe could see that

she was beyond distressed. Terrified that she would never be rid of Sloan.

Unfortunately, that was a very real fear.

She looked at Rafe. "Maybe I need to do what your sister and your bosses want me to."

"Meaning what?"

"Make Oliver believe I want him back and—"

"No way," Rafe said. "Forget it. I already told you, that's not going to happen."

"But couldn't you put a wire on me? If I could get him to admit he set you up, if I could get him to confess to me that he had those Russians killed, wouldn't that be enough to—"

"Did you hear what I just said?" Rafe barked. "The guy's a psychopath. If he were to find out what you're up to... I'm not going to put you in that position."

"Well, maybe it's not your choice," she told him.

"It's the *only* choice, Lisa. Anything else is too dangerous."

She stood up now. "You know, I love you with all my heart, Rafe, but don't for a minute think you can tell me what to do any more than Oliver can. If you think you can control me..."

"I'm trying to *protect* you, Leese."

"And look what it got you," she said. "Maybe it's time I started protecting myself." Then she turned and walked out the door.

Chapter Twenty-Two

They were silent on the ride back to Grandma Natalie's house. The only one who had anything say was Eberhart, who seemed outright gleeful that he had been proven right. That nothing would—or had—come of their little jaunt to the bank.

He said to Rafe, "I'm holding you responsible for all of this, Franco. You're an embarrassment to your entire family."

Kate said, "Shut up, Charlie."

"You telling me I'm wrong? I'll leave it a jury to decide if he offed those two Russians, but you can't deny he's been stickin' his nose in where it don't—"

"Shut. Up. Charlie."

He would have kept going if Kate hadn't given him the death stare. The one she'd been perfecting since she and Rafe were kids.

Rafe had always sensed a lot of tension between her and Eberhart, and was pretty sure that Kate would just as soon trade the guy in for a new partner. But in the Sheriff's department you didn't always have a choice of who you'd be riding with. And unless the relationship was so fractured that the two of you were coming to blows, changing the situation was next to impossible. So you did your best to get along.

Not that Eberhart was making much of an effort. Yet for all his faults, he wasn't wrong. Rafe *was* an embarrassment to the Franco clan, and he'd be the first to admit it.

He just wasn't sure it mattered all that much at this point.

After Kate dropped them off, Rafe and Lisa went inside and Lisa scooped up Chloe in her arms and took her straight to the bedroom, closing the door behind them.

All she said to Rafe was that she had "some thinking to do" and that was that.

End of communication.

HE DIDN'T SEE HER again until close to dinner.

She came down to help Nonna and Bea in the kitchen as he took babysitting duty and watched cartoons with Chloe.

The girl sat close to him on the sofa, snuggling up against him, and Rafe put an arm around her, once again feeling that inexplicable connection.

He wondered if she ever missed her father.

How could she not?

Yet oddly, Chloe had yet to even mention Sloan. Maybe the guy didn't like pink and blue kitty cats.

That was the least of his faults, if true. Sloan didn't strike Rafe as the type to care much about kids, and Rafe had to wonder what his reaction had been when Lisa told him he'd gotten her pregnant.

Joy? Elation?

Doubtful. The only thing Sloan got elated about was Sloan. He was a narcissist, pure and simple, and Rafe didn't get the impression that he'd ever spent more than obligatory time with his daughter.

Which was probably for the best.

Rafe couldn't imagine having a child like this and not wanting to spend as much time as possible with her. If she were his, if he were lucky enough to be her father, she would quickly become the center of his universe.

Kitty cats and all.

BEA DID MOST OF THE TALKING during dinner, telling them stories of her childhood in a small town in Texas. How her father had wanted a boy and had raised her to ride and shoot and wrestle pigs in the mud patch.

Chloe seemed to get a kick out of that one. The thought of this woman rolling around in the mud with a three-hundred-pound pig was too much for the girl to handle, and she giggled like crazy, asking Bea to tell the story again.

Lisa, on the other hand, seemed pensive, barely touching her dinner. Several times, Rafe was tempted to ask her what was going on inside her head, suspecting he already knew, but he resisted.

She would talk when she was ready to.

He thought about what she had said at the bank. About him trying to control her, just as Sloan always had.

Was that true?

If it was, that had never been his intention. Rafe had always had strong opinions, sure, but he wouldn't dream of trying to impose them on anyone, especially Lisa.

But he wouldn't shy away from telling her exactly how he felt, either. And to his mind, playing games with Sloan was far too risky.

HE WAS READING a bedtime story to Chloe when Lisa appeared in the doorway, fresh from a shower, wearing a terry-cloth robe.

"I need to talk to you when you're finished," she said.

She stepped into the room, kissed Chloe on the forehead and bid her good-night, then left them alone so that Rafe could finish the story. It was one his own mother used to read to him about Whacky Wednesday, where everything in the world seemed to have been turned upside down.

He was halfway through it when he realized that Chloe was asleep. Smoothing her hair back, he raised the blanket up to her small chest, then turned out the light and closed the door.

A moment later, he was in Lisa's room, surprised to find her dressed in tight-fitting blue jeans and an equally tight cardigan sweater. Her hair was brushed back and she'd put on enough makeup to enhance but not mar her natural beauty.

"I thought you were getting ready for bed," he said. "What's going on?"

"Sit down, Rafe."

He studied her a moment, saw the measured determination in her eyes, then sat on the edge of the bed.

She moved to him, took his hands. "I'm sorry I got so upset with you at the bank this afternoon. I shouldn't have lashed out at you like that. All you've ever tried to do was help me."

"I'm glad you understand that. But don't even worry about it. You had a right to be upset."

"Maybe, but there's something *you* need to understand. Do you think you can try to do that?"

"Of course," he said.

"Good. Because I have to make this right. You're in trouble because Oliver is obsessed with me. And while there's nothing I can do to control that, I can at least try to stop him."

Rafe stared at her. "You called Kate, didn't you?"

She nodded. "I told her I wasn't bluffing this afternoon. I'm more than willing to cooperate with their investigation and wear a wire. She's setting it up as we speak."

"For tonight?"

She nodded. "I've already asked Oliver to meet me at the house. Alone."

A mix of emotions tore at Rafe and he squeezed her hands. "Lisa, this is crazy."

"I'm not asking for your approval. But if we're ever going to have any kind of life together—and I'd like that, more than anything—then something has to be done about Oliver. Something that will keep him away from us forever."

"And if this goes wrong? What then?"

"I don't see why it should. All I have to do is play to Oliver's weakness—which is me."

"I don't like this, Lisa. You know I don't like it."

"You've made that abundantly clear. But how do we have any kind of relationship if you're doing time in jail? How will you ever get to know your daughter if the only way you see her is through a set of bars?"

The words had gone by so quickly that Rafe thought he must have misunderstood her. When he ran them through his head again, his heart momentarily seized up and he got a lump in his throat.

"My daughter?" He swallowed. "What are you telling me?"

"I wanted you to know three years ago, Rafe. I *should* have told you then, just as I should have told you the moment you walked into my living room and saw her. But I've been so afraid about how you'd react that I kept looking for excuses not to." She paused, moving in close to him. "But I can't keep it from you anymore, Rafe. Chloe isn't Oliver's child. She's yours. Every drop of blood she carries comes from you and me."

Rafe just sat there, staring at her, thinking he surely must have fallen asleep in Chloe's room and was dreaming this entire conversation.

But then he thought of that connection he had with the girl. That feeling of oneness whenever he interacted with her. And he knew this was real. That Lisa spoke the truth.

"Oh, my God," he said. "Oh, my God."

Rafe had never been one for tears—men raised in cop families would rather shoot themselves than ever shed one—but he felt his eyes growing wet. Couldn't have stopped it if he wanted to.

"I'm so sorry I didn't tell you sooner," Lisa said. "Can you ever forgive me?"

"Forgive you? There's nothing to forgive. This is the most wonderful news I've ever heard."

Then he pulled her close, wrapped his arms around her and kissed her.

He was a father.

Better still, he was *Chloe's* father.

But before he could revel in this notion, a

horn honked outside and Lisa said, "I have to go. That'll be Kate and her team. It's time to do this."

Then she kissed him again, pulled herself free and headed for the door.

BY THE TIME Rafe reached the porch, Lisa was climbing through the sliding door of a telephone company van.

"Wait a minute," he called out. "Hold on."

She turned in the doorway. "You're not going to stop me, Rafe. I've made up my mind."

"Fine," he said as he crossed the lawn toward her. "I get that. But if you think you're going to do this without me, you're sadly mistaken."

Now Kate stuck her head out of the van. "Haven't you already gotten yourself in enough trouble? Stay home, little brother."

Rafe looked inside the vehicle and saw one of his cousins at the wheel, a St. Louis police officer named Billy Franco. In back with Kate was Mike Cuddy, a family friend and a freelance audio surveillance technician unconnected to the Sheriff's department.

In other words, neither of them were part of Kate's usual crew.

"What's going on here?" he asked. "Where's your partner? This doesn't look like a sanctioned operation."

"Don't you worry about that," she said.

"You haven't even passed this by the brass, have you? And you know Eberhart would blow the whistle if you tried to bring him in on it."

"I don't have time to deal with protocol. They always tie us up with endless planning and I just got word from one of my informants that Sloan may be gearing up to leave town on a business deal. I don't want to lose momentum."

"Or take a chance that Lisa will change her mind?"

"I'm not changing anything," Lisa said.

"Well, you're not doing this without me, either," Rafe told her, then looked pointedly at Kate. "Either you let me come along or I blow the whole operation."

Kate studied him with a scowl as if he were the pesky little brother threatening to tell their parents what she was up to. Then she said, "Well, then, don't just stand there, you little twerp. Get inside."

A moment later, they were on their way.

As BILLY DROVE THEM through the city streets, Mike had Lisa remove her sweater and began wiring up her bra. A tiny microphone was attached to the fabric between her cleavage, with a lead running to a compact wireless transmitter taped to the small of her back.

When she put the sweater back on, it was impossible to tell she was wired at all. As long as Sloan kept his hands to himself, she would be safe.

But then there was no guarantee of that, was there?

"Okay," Kate told her. "These are the rules."

"I'm listening."

"First of all, you have to relax when you're with him. If he senses you're wearing a wire, if you offer him any kind of tell, you could find yourself in a very dangerous situation."

"Which is exactly what I'm afraid of," Rafe said.

Kate scowled again. "We've heard enough from you, buddy boy. You're either along for the ride or you get out now. Your choice."

She was once again pulling the big sister card, and under different circumstances Rafe may well have told her where to stuff it. But he said nothing.

She returned her attention to Lisa. "Now, when it comes to coaxing information out of this guy, you have to remember that he's been around the block a few times and won't be easily fooled."

"I was married to him, remember? I think I can handle him."

"Let's hope so, because we don't have time for me to instruct you in the finer art of extracting a confession. The thing you've got going for you is that the guy is apparently nuts about you."

"Or just plain nuts," Rafe said.

Kate ignored him and continued addressing Lisa. "When you called him, did you say what I told you to?"

Lisa nodded. "I told him that I thought things had gotten a little out of control and I wanted to talk. No promises. No enticements."

"Good. Because he'd probably be suspicious otherwise. Especially after a year of making it clear that you want nothing to do with him."

"I don't think he's suspicious at all," Lisa said. "I think this has led exactly where he wanted it to. My needing something from him. And a chance to put us in the same room without my threatening to call the police."

"Let's hope you're right," Kate said, then turned to Mike and gestured to Lisa's chest. "What's the range on this thing?"

"We should be able to get a clear signal up to a block or so away."

She turned again to Lisa. "Okay. We can't very well drop you off in front of your house, so we're going to drive to a cabstand and let you ride the last mile home. But don't worry, we'll be parked about a half block south of your place, and we can hear every word you and Sloan say."

"And what if things go wrong?" Rafe said. "What's the emergency phrase?"

Lisa looked confused. "Emergency phrase?"

"A phrase that lets us know when it's time to move in," Kate said. "When you feel as if your life is in danger. Something that's unlikely to come up in normal conversation."

They all thought about this for a moment, then Rafe said, "How about pink and blue kitty cats?"

"Not one I would have chosen," Kate told him, "but it works as well as any." She looked at Lisa. "So that's the phrase. Pink and blue kitty cats. You think you can remember it?"

Lisa smiled and threw a glance at Rafe. "I'm sure I'll manage," she said.

Chapter Twenty-Three

When the cab dropped her off in front of the house, Lisa felt her knees shaking. She'd have to get that under control if she was going to make this work.

What she hadn't bothered to tell either Kate or Rafe, was that Oliver had always been a keen observer of human behavior, which was part of the reason he was so successful in business.

And Kate had been right. If he sensed even the slightest hesitation in Lisa's manner, she was done for. The choking incident from the other day was only a preview of coming attractions.

The one thing Lisa had on her side, however, was Oliver's ego. He was the type of guy with the kind of money that attracted women far and wide. And he was just vain enough to believe that it was *him* they wanted, and not the lifestyle he promised them.

The irony was that Lisa had never been much interested in that lifestyle. Money only served a purpose—putting food in her daughter's stomach and giving them shelter. Anything other than that was superfluous nonsense that held no real meaning for her.

It was Oliver's initial kindness that had attracted her to him, and the promise that he would take care of her and Chloe when they most needed taking care of. And on some level, it saddened her that things had gone sour.

But that sadness paled compared to the feeling of revulsion she now felt whenever she thought of him. She just hoped she'd be able to use that giant ego against him and get him to confess to his crimes.

When she got inside the house, she immediately turned on the lights in the living room, then went upstairs for a moment to get something she needed.

By the time she came back down, she heard a car pull into the driveway. She had asked Oliver to come alone and hoped he had followed her wishes.

When she peeked out the window, she saw him emerge from behind the wheel of his Lexus and head for the front door.

A moment later, the bell chimed, and Lisa took a deep breath, tried to steady her knees… then went to the door to greet him.

"HEY, BABE," Sloan said. "I was starting to wonder if this day would ever come."

His voice came in crystal clear over the wire. Whatever microphone and transmitter Mike had used, it had to be top of the line.

Rafe sat next to Kate inside the cramped van, listening carefully through a pair of headphones. He'd gotten a knot in his stomach the moment Sloan rang the front doorbell, and he didn't figure it would go away until this whole thing was over.

He had checked and rechecked his spare weapon to make sure it was loaded. Had done it so many times that Kate had finally put a hand on his wrist and told him to "Chill out, little brother."

"You're looking as hot as ever," Sloan said. "The way you're wearing that sweater, I'd almost think you're glad to see me. So are you gonna invite me in or what?"

"I'm surprised you haven't forced your way in."

She was playing it smart. Showing him that

she was still upset. Anything else would seem false and give him reason to be suspicious.

"Hey," he said. "I was a little loaded, okay? I had something to celebrate, so I was celebrating."

LISA NOTICED the twinkle in Oliver's eye and knew exactly what he was talking about.

"Let me guess," she said. "You were celebrating your little victory at the Westland National Bank."

Oliver smiled. "Looks like somebody took a field trip. Guess you didn't find what you were looking for, did you?"

"You know I didn't," Lisa said. "But I'm not going to stand here and cry about it. You might as well come in."

She opened the door wide and let him pass. He brushed a shoulder against her breasts as he did, a tiny smirk on his lips.

And here we go, she thought, figuring Rafe and the others must have heard the scrape on the microphone and gone into a panic.

She quickly said, "Have a seat. Do you want a drink?"

Sloan smiled and crossed to the sofa. "When's the last time you ever saw me turn down anything you had to offer? Like I told you the other night, babe. You pretty much drive me crazy."

"I take it that means yes?" She moved to the wet bar in the corner.

"Vodka rocks. Same as always."

She put some ice in a glass, poured the liquid in, then turned and carried it to him. He was already sprawled out on the sofa, the king making himself at home in his castle.

The way he had his legs splayed she could clearly see the bulge in his pants. This was, she knew, a deliberate show, as if to say to her, *Look what you've been missing.*

Lisa stifled an involuntary urge to vomit all over him and handed him the drink.

He took a sip, then looked up at her. "You gonna stand there all night showing off that glorious rack, or tell me why I'm here? Not that I'm complaining, mind you."

"I'm surprised you don't already know," she said. "You seem to know everything else."

He grinned. "I do my best. But I've gotta say I was a little bowled over when my attorney told me about your cop friend."

"Oh? And what did she tell you?"

"She showed me pictures of the two of you in college. Quite the pretty little couple you were." He took a sip. "We sat there and did the math. Figured out when school ended, when you two parted ways—and the next thing I know, I realize I'm looking at a picture of Chloe's father."

She wondered what Rafe was thinking right now. She was relieved he had taken the news so well, but figured he might not be too happy with the subtle sneer in Oliver's tone.

"And that disturbs you?" she asked. She didn't really care one way or another, but she wanted him to feel relaxed. As if he could share anything with her.

Oliver shrugged. "I honestly don't give a rat's behind who knocked you up. But when he shows up in your life again and winds up storming into my hotel room all hot and bothered over something he thinks I did to you, I might have an issue or two about that."

"What kind of an issue?"

"Maybe I don't like the guy moving in on my woman."

Lisa shook her head. "You don't own me, Oliver. We're divorced, remember?"

"Only because you forced it on me. I figure I show a little kindness to a pregnant girl in need, give her a home, some clothes, welcome her kid into the world—"

"You didn't even come to the hospital."

"What can I say? I was busy. The point is, I *do* own you, Lisa. I own you just like I own that car out in the driveway, and all the people who work for me. Just like I own that cop boyfriend of yours, now that he's seen how the law really works."

Lisa laughed. "Don't you realize how pitiful that is?"

"What's that suppose to mean?"

"Think about it, Oliver. You say you own me, but in order to get me to pay any attention to you, you have to frame an innocent man. Yet the one thing you can't control is how I feel."

Oliver shrugged. "Feelings are overrated."

"So what is it you want from me? Is it the body?" She laughed. "You could walk into a nightclub, waggle your finger and half the women in St. Louis would come running. And most of them are better built than me."

"It isn't the body," Sloan said, "It's the way you use it. But even if they could give you competition in that department, they still wouldn't be you, would they now?"

"What's so special about me?"

Sloan chuckled, took another sip of his drink. "To be perfectly honest, babe, I have no idea. There's just something about you that turns me on. Always has, always will. And I figure if I can't have you, nobody else can, either."

"So is that why you framed Rafe Franco?"

A slow grin. "That's the second time you've said that, and I have no idea what you're talking about."

"I didn't just throw that data chip into my safety deposit box without looking at it first, Oliver. I saw what was on it. I saw names. And one of them was Azarov. The same guy Rafe is accused of killing."

"Well, isn't that a coincidence."

"No," Lisa said, "I don't think it is."

Oliver stared at her for a long moment, then knocked back the last of his vodka and held out the glass. "Hit me again, will you?"

Oh, I'd like to hit you all right, she thought, her frustration mounting.

Was she ever going to get him to admit to anything, or was she wasting her time?

She took his glass, then crossed back to the wet bar and poured more liquid over the ice.

"You know," he said, "I've gotta thank you for taking that stuff off my computer. I thought I was some kind of Mr. Wizard, keeping that folder hidden, but I figured if my own wife could find it, maybe the cops could, too. Which is why I decided to wipe my hard drive, just in case you got chatty."

"I could have gotten chatty a long time ago," she told him. "But I didn't, did I? All I wanted was for you to leave me and Chloe alone."

"And all I've ever wanted is you, in this house, on your knees, in my bed, doing what I tell you to do when I tell you to do it, without complaint. So I guess we've got a bit of a problem, don't we?" He gestured. "You gonna bring me that drink or what?"

She crossed to the sofa, handed it to him. He tipped it back, drinking half of it down.

"What if I told you you could have that?" she said. "Me at your beck and call."

He stopped, gulped. Looked at her. "Is this some kind of trick?"

"No tricks, Oliver. A straight-up proposition. A business deal, if you will."

He furrowed his brow. "Business deal, huh? Are we finally getting to the meat of the matter? Is that why you invited me here?"

"Yes," she said.

She got down on her knees in front of him, framed by those splayed legs, then leaned forward and kissed him full on the mouth.

THEY HEARD THE RUSTLE of fabric accompanied by nothing but silence and Rafe knew she had to be kissing him.

What else could it be?

He and Kate exchanged glances as he racked and reracked the gun in his hand, wanting desperately to use it.

"What the heck is she doing?" he said to Kate.

"Quiet. She's playing this perfectly. Just let her do her thing."

He was about ready to throw the rear doors open, run the half block to Lisa's house and barge in firing, when Sloan broke the silence.

"Well, well," he said. "Looks like you've still got the magic, babe. Not that I ever doubted it. But I have to admit I'm a little surprised."

"Why? It's what you wanted, isn't it?"

"That and a whole lot more."

"Well, that's what I'm offering," she said. "Me. The whole package. I'll even pretend I care about you sometimes."

Rafe squirmed. Was this part of the script Lisa had planned or was she simply improvising?

"In exchange for what?" Sloan asked.

"Rafe Franco," she said.

ANOTHER SLOW SMILE came to Oliver's face. "Rafe Franco, huh? You want to illuminate me on this little demand?"

She kissed him again, lingering for a moment, mentally holding her nose as she flicked her tongue along his lower lip.

Then she said, "Doesn't matter what you admit to. I know you framed him."

"You ever gonna stop singing that tune?"

"You're a powerful man, Oliver, and you get things done. I don't care whose arm you have to twist, who you have to bribe, but you're going to do whatever you have to do to get the charges against him dropped."

Sloan chuckled. "You're giving me a lot more credit than I deserve."

"Really?" she said. "I thought you were the man who owned everything."

"Well, sure, but…"

Another kiss. This one longer, deeper. Lisa nearly gagged halfway through it.

Then Oliver reached forward and cupped her breast, running his thumb over the fabric, feeling the thin bra beneath, and the nipple beneath that. She felt a momentary stab of panic, worried he might find the microphone, but he wasn't anywhere close.

No, he was sticking to that one specific

spot. She thought she might have to will her body to react, but the friction finally did its job and she grew harder against it.

She could feel *his* body growing harder as well, his splayed legs now pressed up against her abdomen. She halfway hoped that Rafe had taken his headphones off by now. He may not be getting a visual, but she didn't want him hearing this and letting his imagination go wild.

"You must really care about this guy," Oliver said.

"He's the father of my child. I don't want him to see her grow up from behind bars."

"You sure you don't want more than that?"

"That's all it *can* be, if you agree to my terms."

He kept working that thumb, and it took everything Lisa had not to flinch away from him.

"I wish I could, babe, believe me. But you've got me all wrong. I'm no fan of the guy, by any means, but I'm just a real estate developer. I don't have the kind of juice it takes to set him up *or* smooth it all out."

"Come on, Oliver, how stupid do you think I am? I saw those files, remember?"

"You saw some names and numbers," he said. "Doesn't mean a thing."

"So is that why you went to all the trouble of finding it? Of having someone pose as me to get it?"

"I'll have to plead the fifth on that one."

She reached forward and ran a hand along the side of his jaw, caressing it. "Are you going to plead the fifth on the man in the BMW, too?"

Sloan frowned. "I beg your pardon?"

"He came after us, Oliver. Shot at Rafe. He could have killed me, too. Probably would have, if he hadn't been hit by a truck. Are you going to tell me you didn't hire him?"

All of a sudden Sloan's face got ugly and his forefinger joined his thumb, pinching her nipple between them—hard. Sharp, searing pain shot through Lisa's breast and she stifled a cry, not wanting Rafe to know what was happening.

She didn't want him coming in here just yet.

"I don't know what you think you're playing at, you little slut, but you're treading on dangerous ground."

He bore down and the pain was relentless, and in that moment Lisa knew that this attempt at getting Oliver to talk had been an exercise in futility. That the only way she'd ever get this man out of her life was to take a page from *his* book. A contingency she had planned for when she went upstairs.

Wincing against the pain, she reached forward and shoved her right hand under the sofa cushion. She found what she had hidden there, pulled it free and pointed it directly at Oliver's forehead.

The gun from the upstairs closet.

Oliver's face went slack and he immediately released her. "Now wait a second, babe, you want to be very careful with that thing."

Lisa got to her feet and held the gun with both hands now, keeping it trained on Oliver, who looked as if he were about to pee his pants.

Then she said, "Pink and blue kitty cats."

Chapter Twenty-Four

The words came so suddenly that no one in the van had expected them. A split second after Lisa spoke, she yelped loudly and three gunshots rang out.

Bam. Bam. Bam.

Rafe ripped his headphones off and bolted. Flew out of the van as if he had been launched by a catapult, covering the half block to her house in marathon time, his heart pounding, working its way up into his throat.

He heard footsteps behind him and knew Kate and the others were following his lead. A moment later, he crashed through the front door, gun high, expecting to find Lisa on the floor…

But to his surprise, the living room was empty.

What the heck?

"Fan out," Kate said behind him. "Check every room."

They moved quickly and efficiently, Rafe keeping his weapon extended as he moved down a hallway dotted with doors. He went room to room, kicking each door open, shouting "Clear!" when he saw that they were empty.

He heard more shouts of "Clear!" coming from other parts of the house, and when he'd checked every room he could find, he headed back to the living room where their cousin Billy was now waiting.

"I got nothing," Billy said.

"Same here," Kate told them, as she came down the stairs.

Rafe shook his head in disbelief. "This doesn't make any sense. Where did they go?"

"In here!" Mike shouted, and they all ran toward the sound of his voice, moving down another short hallway that led into what looked like a study. There was a desk in front of the window and floor-to-ceiling bookshelves full of hardback books.

Mike was standing near the center of the wall, pulling on one of the books. "They're fake," he said, then pressed inward on a panel and a section of the bookcase sprang open, revealing a door behind. "It's an escape route.

It was hanging open when I came into the room."

Rafe was about to step into the hidden passage, when they heard the sound of an engine roaring.

The Lexus.

Sloan's Lexus.

Turning, Rafe rocketed out of the room and headed toward the sound, crossing the living room to the foyer in seconds flat. He burst onto the front driveway with his weapon raised, only to see the Lexus roaring onto the street, burning rubber as it went.

He ran for all he was worth, trying to catch up to it, but by the time he reached the bottom of the driveway it was halfway down the street.

Rafe pointed his gun at it, but he knew that taking a shot would be foolish. A tiny miscalculation and Lisa could get hurt—because Rafe knew damn well she was inside.

Kate and the others drew up beside him as the Lexus screamed around a corner and disappeared into the night.

Then he turned to his big sister and said angrily, "No time to deal with protocol, huh? How's that working for you now?"

LISA AWAKENED with a start, her head pounding, and realized they were in Oliver's Lexus.

And they were moving. Fast.

But before she could move herself, Oliver shot a hand to her throat and grabbed it, squeezing hard. "You try anything, babe, I won't hesitate to hurt you. So be good, okay?"

The pain was excruciating and she struggled to breathe. When he loosened his grip, she sucked big gasps of air, feeling as if she couldn't get enough.

She felt dizzy, her head still pounding, and it took her a moment to remember what had happened.

The gun. She had pulled the gun on Oliver. Because she'd known that was the only way. The only way that she and Chloe—and Rafe—would be rid of him.

It was an irrational move—she knew that now—but her fear had gotten the better of her. If she hadn't hesitated, if she hadn't taken just a split second to consider the weight of what she was doing, Oliver would be dead now. There was no doubt in her mind.

But she *had* hesitated. Pointing a gun at someone—someone you despise—is one thing. But pulling the trigger is another thing altogether, and in that hesitation, Oliver had seen an opening and pounced. Sprang from the sofa and tackled her. The gun was knocked upward and she had involuntarily fired off three shots.

Bam. Bam. Bam.

Then her head had hit something solid—the edge of the coffee table?—and the blow had sent her reeling, spinning away into darkness.

Now here she was in Oliver's car, struggling to breathe, her neck raw where he had grabbed her, and all she could think to say was, "Pink and blue kitty cats. Pink and blue kitty cats. *Pink and blue kitty—*"

"What's wrong with you?" Oliver barked as they barreled down a city street at top speed. "Why do you keep..."

He stopped himself, his face shifting expressions as if he suddenly understood.

"The cops," he said, his eyes going cold. "That's a code phrase. You've been working with the cops."

Then, without warning, he reached a hand out—the same hand that had grabbed her throat—and shoved it up inside her sweater, groping around until he found the transmitter taped to the small of her back.

"You little..."

Grabbing hold of it, he ripped it free, then rolled down his window and tossed it into the street. Shooting her a warning look, he reached into his pocket for a cell phone and hit speed dial.

When the line came alive, he said, "I've got myself a situation that I need you to take care of. Tell those new guys you hired that they're about to earn their keep."

Then he snapped the phone shut and hit the gas.

RAFE WAS BESIDE HIMSELF, couldn't stand still. He paced Lisa's living room like an expectant father worried about bad news.

They had searched for signs of blood, but found none, and could only assume that the gunshots had gone wild. That Lisa had not been hurt.

A least Rafe hoped so.

Prayed for it.

But that didn't change the fact that Lisa was gone.

"He's got her, Kate. You know he's got her. The question is where is he taking her?"

Kate was still studying the carpet. "Maybe *he* doesn't even know," she said. "I've put out an APB on the Lexus and sent some deputies to his hotel. But somehow I have a feeling that's the last place he'll go. Especially if he's on to us."

"If he wasn't before," Rafe said, "he will be as soon as he discovers that wire. Then all bets are off. I can't believe I was stupid enough to let you do this."

"Look, Rafe, I'm sorry, but there's always a risk with this kind of—"

"Risk?" he shouted. "We're talking about the woman I love, Kate, not some confidential informant you've been cultivating for years. This is an unmitigated disaster. And if anything happens to her, I'm holding you responsible."

Kate got to her feet. "Nothing's going to happen, little brother. I promise you."

"Oh? Another promise you can't keep?"

"Maybe we're overthinking this. Maybe she got hurt in the struggle and he's taking her to the hospital."

Rafe stared at her. "You can't be serious. The guy's a narcissistic sociopath."

"I'm just trying to think of all the possibilities, okay? I'm doing the best I can here. So will you please stop pacing and sit down?"

Rafe stared at her a long moment, then moved to sofa and sat. "You happy now?"

He buried his head in his hands. Why had he given in to this nonsense so easily? Why had he allowed Lisa to do something so foolish? If anything happened to her, if Sloan were to hurt her in any way, he'd never forgive himself.

He looked at his sister again. "We need to figure out where he's taking her, Kate. The longer she's with him, the better the chance he'll…"

Rafe stopped suddenly, saw something from the corner of his eye. Getting to his feet, he moved to the end table at the far end of the couch and found a framed photograph there, the glass broken.

"What is it?" Kate asked.

Rafe picked up the photo. It was one he had seen before, the shot of Lisa and Chloe standing in front of a house on a lake.

Carlyle Lake.

It's the only time in our marriage that we were actually happy, Lisa had said.

Kate moved toward him. "Rafe? What is it?"

He turned now and showed her the photograph.

"I think I know where he's taking her."

Chapter Twenty-Five

It was a family operation.

Following protocol meant mobilizing an entire division, and with that came endless questions and wasted time spent debating whether or not the taxpayers should be paying for the search and rescue of someone who might not even be missing. Especially when that search and rescue required crossing state lines.

Considering that this problem had been caused by an unauthorized operation, the prudent decision was to handle the matter in-house—or in-family, so to speak—rather than put the brass in a bind should things go wrong. So Rafe, Kate, Billy and Mike were joined by Billy's brother, Mario, and Rafe and Kate's older brother, Vincent.

They convened in Lisa's living room, where Mario—who headed a cybercrime task force for the FBI—used a backdoor channel to hack into Oliver Sloan's real estate records.

"So what am I looking for?" he asked.

Rafe said, "Any properties he may own in Carlyle, Illinois."

Mario spent the next several minutes stabbing keys on his laptop keyboard, then said, "Got something. Looks like an acre of land right off the lakefront."

"That's the one," Kate told him, then looked at Rafe. "If you're right about this, looks like we're back in business."

CALLING IT A LAKE HOUSE was something of a misnomer. According to the blueprints Mario downloaded, it was more of a compound than a house, and judging by the way Sloan had protected himself at the hotel, Rafe figured there would be plenty of security there.

Rather than go in guns blazing, and risk hurting Lisa in the process, they decided on a stealth assault, using the darkness to shield them. The trick was to get inside undetected and extract Lisa from the premises.

"We'll want to go for maximum coverage," Vincent said. He was the oldest of the clan and took charge immediately. His job as a squad commander required him to make a dozen different decisions every day. "With six of us working in pairs, we can come in from three different entry points." He pointed to the blueprint. "Here, here and here."

"What about security?" Rafe asked.

"It's my understanding that this clown Sloan is known for using over-the-hill mercenaries. But we shouldn't be overconfident. Some of these guys are very good at what they do."

"Do we use deadly force?" Billy asked.

"Only if necessary. There's no question they'll be ordered to shoot to kill, but let's do our best to neutralize them quietly. That leaves fewer questions to answer later on. So we're talking maximum efficiency, minimum violence."

Good luck with that one, Rafe thought. Once Sloan got wind of them, all bets were off.

"All right," Vincent said, pointing again to the blueprint. "Kate, you partner with Rafe and take the west flank. Billy and Mike you come in here, from the north. Covering the lakefront requires a boat, so we'll forgo that potential snafu and Mario and I will enter from the south flank." He looked at them.

"Assuming she's in there, this should be over in a few short minutes."

"What about Sloan?" Kate said. "How do we handle him?"

Rafe's face hardened. "Just leave him to me."

HE PUT HER IN their old bedroom at the back of the main house. It had been a good year or so since Lisa had been here, and despite what their marriage had become, her memories of the place were fond ones.

Most of the time they'd spent here had been in the early days, shortly after they'd said their vows and Lisa still believed she had married a good man who wanted only to protect her and the child she would soon give birth to.

But that man had long since disappeared, only to be replaced by the creature who had brought her here, for reasons known only to him.

Was this his safe haven? His protection from the outside world and the people who were looking for her?

Or did he hope to recapture something here? Somehow find what they had lost so long ago?

It seemed to Lisa that Oliver had lost so much more than a marriage. In these past few hours, she realized that he had also lost his mind. He hid it well with his charm and his good looks and his easy smile, but beneath that exterior was a monster whose only desire was to make her bend to his will.

It would almost be comic, if she weren't a victim of it. But she now had bruises on her throat and a sore, aching breast that proved what Oliver was capable of when provoked.

And it didn't seem to take much to provoke him.

Just before he locked her in the room, he had thrown one of her old negligees at her feet and told her to put it on.

"I've got plans for us tonight, babe. A little stroll down memory lane."

The thought filled Lisa with revulsion. And when he was gone, she stared at the negligee and told herself that no matter what Oliver did, no matter how much he hurt her, she would never bend, never break, never give him the satisfaction of letting him touch her that way again.

Not voluntarily, at least.

And if he tried, she'd break his neck.

THEY DROVE TO CARLYLE in the telephone company van, each of them lost in their own thoughts, remaining silent, as if the utterance of a single word might somehow jinx them.

When they found the compound, to no one's surprise it was lit up, signaling that the place was in full operation.

Parking in the shadows of a tree, several yards from the gated front entrance, Vincent leveled a pair of binoculars at the drive and said, "Bingo. We've got ourselves a Lexus."

Rafe felt his heartbeat quicken. His instincts had been right. Lisa was inside.

Please be inside.

There was a high stone fence and a lot of foliage surrounding the compound. A uniformed security guard stood near the gate with watchful eyes, undoubtedly warned to keep a lookout for the police. Any approach would be turned away with demands for a warrant—something Rafe and crew were unable to provide.

But the sight of this telephone company truck—if the guard had, indeed, seen them— did not seem to arouse any suspicions.

Pulling out of the shadows, they did a single sweep around the compound to assess their options and confirm that the blueprints had been accurate. There were no neighboring houses for several hundred yards, and they decided the isolation could only work in their favor.

Rafe and Kate were dropped off near the west quadrant, both carrying an extra weapon, a miniature flashlight and a lightweight headset that Mike had set them up with. Rafe wished he had a pair of night goggles, to boot, but this was a run-and-gun operation and they weren't exactly swimming in taxpayer-funded supplies.

The fence was about eight feet high. Rafe gave Kate a boost up, then she, in turn, pulled him up after. They each peered into the darkness and saw a wide stretch of lawn that led first to a guest cottage, then on to the main house beyond, and were relieved to see the area free of dog droppings.

Either the cleanup crew was very good at its job, or guard dogs had been forfeited in favor of manpower.

Earlier, they had discussed the possibility of alarm sensors, but a search of Sloan's credit card records—courtesy of a computer hack by Mario—showed no signs of any security company purchases in the past ten years.

Rafe and Kate waited a tense moment, in

case their presence had been detected, then dropped to the ground inside the compound and darted toward the shadows of a nearby shade tree.

Rafe scanned the yard and saw no sign of a guard until his gaze fell on the main house. There were two men posted out front, and he assumed there would be more teams posted at the sides and in the back.

Kate gestured toward another shade tree, which was only a yard or so from the guest-house. They waited until both security men had turned away, then took off, making a bee-line for the shadows.

As they crouched down, Kate assessed their surroundings and said quietly, "I'm figuring at least eight hostiles at the main house and possibly a couple of outliers on patrol."

"Exactly what I was thinking," Rafe told her.

Kate touched her headset. "Team leader, we've only got two hostiles in sight, but have to assume there are more."

The radio crackled in Rafe's ear and Vincent said, "Roger, Kate, we can confirm two on our end."

"Same here," Billy said. "And we came very

close to an encounter with a patrol jockey on the way in."

"Did they spot you?" Vincent asked.

"They would've lit the place up if they had."

"All right," Vincent said. "Let's do this the smart way. One man handles the security detail, the other takes the house. Move quickly and efficiently, and no screwups, or the hostage could wind up dead."

Rafe didn't like the sound of that, but he knew Vincent was right. He turned to Kate and they spoke quietly for a moment, agreeing that Kate would handle the guards.

A moment later, they were moving again, headed for the main house.

Chapter Twenty-Six

Sloan wanted to kill something.

It was just that simple.

Ever since Lisa had told him that the hit man he'd hired had not only failed to do his job, but also had been hit by a truck, a nearly uncontrollable feeling of anger had risen inside him.

If the hit man had gotten himself killed, what had he left behind?

Was this something Sloan needed to be worried about?

His attorney, Berletti, had repeatedly insisted on the phone that there were no links to him, but Sloan had learned a long time ago—back in his early Chicago days—that if you relied on other people to do your dirty work, mistakes were sometimes made. And those mistakes could come back to bite *you* instead of the idiot who made them.

But as disturbing as this news may have

been, it was nothing compared to the fact that Rafe Franco was still alive. Sloan had been promised that once the man was thoroughly humiliated and his reputation destroyed, he would become worm food.

But that hadn't happened. Franco was still out there somewhere, probably looking for Lisa at this very moment. Because Sloan knew the deputy had to be behind the little sting operation she had tried to pull. He had probably been the one to talk her into it.

And that was the thing that angered him most of all. That Lisa had *allowed* herself to be manipulated like that, had even pulled a *gun* on him—and had actually tried to use it.

Here he had given this witch his heart, and she had been treating him like dirt, like used tissue, from the moment they'd met. She wasn't just a gold digger, she was a cold-hearted tart who deserved to suffer some very serious pain before he snuffed her out for good.

Maybe if she was dead, he'd be able to forget about her. Maybe if she was dead, this uncontrollable feeling of yearning and lust he felt whenever he thought of her would go away. Because he desperately needed it to go away.

Sloan couldn't understand what it was about Lisa that cut so deep. He had slept with a hundred different women in his time, but he'd never had this feeling before. This sense of complete powerlessness.

And that scared him more than any thug with a gun could ever come close to.

Sloan sat in his kitchen, anger coursing through him, staring at a row of prescription bottles lined up on the table in front of him. He had seven doctors on retainer, and the narcotic cocktails they gave him helped dull the edge he often felt.

But they couldn't quell the anger.

Not this time.

Knocking back his fourth vodka rocks, he slammed the glass on the table and got to his feet. He'd been sitting here stewing long enough. Lisa should have packed that dynamite body of hers into the negligee by now, and he planned to teach her a lesson before he killed her. Reduce her to a simpering mass of human waste and make her beg for mercy before he did the final deed.

Then maybe he could get some rest.

Maybe the anger would disappear.

Maybe this ache would go away once and for all.

WHEN KATE GAVE HIM the signal, Rafe darted across the lawn toward the side of the main house. The two security men posted near the door there had foolishly let down their guard, and Kate had taken the opportunity to sneak up behind them and neutralize them quickly and quietly.

Now Rafe was heading through the door, gun in hand, hoping there wouldn't be any surprises inside.

But the moment he got it closed behind him, he heard the faint rustle of fabric as another security man closed in on him. Whirling around, Rafe grabbed a handful of the guy's shirt, jerked him forward, then spun him and put him in a choke hold.

A moment later, the guy was on the floor, out cold.

Although Rafe had looked at the blueprints and had a general sense of how to navigate this house, there were unknown variables at work here. He had no idea how many more of these monkeys he'd have to deal with.

He scanned the area around him and saw that he was in the mudroom, a drain in the floor, a sink and hose in the corner, jackets and boots hung on hooks in the wall.

Beyond this would be a long hallway that,

to the left, led to a massive living room and kitchen. To the right were three of the seven bedrooms the house boasted, including the master, all the way in back.

Rafe figured Lisa could be in any one of these rooms. But knowing where they were located was one thing, and getting to them without sounding any alarms, was another thing altogether. His only sense of comfort was that Vincent and crew were bound to be in the house, as well.

To confirm this, he touched the button on his headset three times—the signal that he'd made it inside unscathed. A moment later, the signal came back, and he knew the game was on.

Pulling open a closet, he stuffed the security man inside, then moved to the doorway adjacent to the hall and carefully peeked around the threshold, checking both ends for any sign of hostile activity.

Seeing that it was clear, he stepped into the hallway and went to work.

LISA WAS STANDING at the window when the door opened behind her. She had thought for a moment that she saw movement out there. Someone slipping through the shadows. And for that split second, her heart had kicked up, a feeling of hope welling up inside her.

It was Rafe out there. It had to be. She knew he wouldn't rest until he found her.

But the hope died the moment she went to the window and saw nothing but the vast expanse of lawn, empty and untouched, lit by the lights from the compound and what little moon there was in the sky.

Then the door opened behind her and she turned, her heart sinking as Oliver stepped into the room.

There was a glassiness to his eyes that she immediately recognized. He was drunk and stoned and angry, and that had never led to anything good in their lives.

He was holding a gun. He let it dangle casually at his side, then used it to gesture to the negligee still lying on the floor.

"I thought I told you to put that on," he said flatly. "And when I tell you something you're supposed to do it."

Lisa eyed him defiantly.

"Or what?" she said. "You're going to shoot me?"

Oliver smiled drunkenly. "I'm saving that for later. Once you've admitted to me how much you love me. How you can't live without me. Which, come to think of it, is pretty much true."

"Go to hell," she told him.

"Yeah?" He moved toward her, raising the gun. He grabbed hold of her arm and twisted it, jerking her forward, pressing the barrel against her forehead. "The way I see it, that's already where you are. The bullet is just a formality."

Lisa struggled, wincing in pain. "Let go of me," she cried.

He pressed the barrel harder and she could feel it denting her skin. "You like that, babe? You like having this smoke stick poking at you? Or maybe you're interested in another kind of stick. Believe me, that can be arranged."

He released her arm and shoved her to the floor. Then he kicked at the negligee, flipping it toward her.

"Put it on," he said.

But she shook her head. "No."

He crouched next to her and pressed the gun against her forehead again.

"Put. It. *On*."

"You're sick, you know that? You need help, Oliver. You're so drugged up and angry you don't even know what you're doing anymore. Why don't you let me help you?"

The offer seemed to surprise him, and he lowered the gun.

"Help me?" he said. "You want to help me? Is that what you were thinking when you drew a gun on me in our living room? You were gonna *help* me?"

"You were hurting me and I panicked," she said. "I didn't even realize what I was doing."

"If you think that was pain, Leese, you've got no concept of what real pain is. Now take those clothes off and get into this negligee, or you'll feel pain you've never in your life knew existed."

"You can't control me, Oliver. I won't do it. And nothing you can do to me will change my mind."

He nodded slowly. "We'll see about that," he said, then got to his feet again. "I grew up in Chicago, babe, and I learned from the best. Men who make the torture specialists for the CIA look like amateurs." He grinned. "By the time I get done with you, you'll be begging me to let you put that thing on. This is gonna be a night to re—"

Lisa lashed out suddenly, driving a fist straight into Oliver's kneecap. He howled and stumbled back, grabbing for it as Lisa jumped to her feet and swept past him, heading straight for the bedroom door.

But Oliver spun around and grabbed her by the hair, jerking her back with such force that she thought her scalp might come loose.

Pain rocketed through her skull. She grabbed at her head as Oliver pulled her backward into the room and spun her around again, pushing her toward the bed.

She sprawled across it and saw the white-hot heat in his eyes. A fury so intense that all rational thought had abandoned him, leaving nothing behind but the reptile. The animal brain.

"You just made a very bad mistake," he said. "A very bad—"

"Sloan!" a voice shouted as the door burst open behind him. And to Lisa's utter joy and relief, Rafe was standing in the doorway, gun raised, zeroed in on Oliver's back.

Oliver froze in place. Didn't move.

"Drop the weapon," Rafe told him. "Now!"

But Oliver didn't seem to hear him. As if he had disappeared inside himself and had lost all communication with the outside world.

"Do it now, Sloan! Or I'll put one in your back!"

Oliver finally nodded, and started to move. Crouching toward the floor, he lowered the gun to lay it on the carpet. But was only half-way there when Lisa saw something deadly flicker in his eyes.

Then suddenly he brought the gun up again, whirled around toward Rafe—

"*Die,* you son of a—"

And Rafe had no choice but to fire.

One. Twice. Three times.

The bullets punctured Oliver's chest and knocked him backward. He landed in a heap at the foot of the bed and didn't move.

Rafe stepped forward quickly, kicked the gun aside, looked at Lisa on the bed.

"I don't think I've ever been so scared for someone in my life," he said. "Are you okay?"

And that was when tears sprang into Lisa's eyes. She launched herself toward Rafe and fell into his arms.

Chapter Twenty-Seven

The wedding took place on a Sunday morning in June.

They held the ceremony in Grandma Natalie's backyard, the entire Franco clan in attendance.

Rafe's brother, Vincent, served as best man, and Beatrice—dressed in her Sunday best—stood in as maid of honor.

The ceremony was brief and sweet. Lisa wore a beautiful lace chiffon wedding gown that was taken out of mothballs and dry-cleaned for the occasion by Grandma Natalie. It was the very same dress Nonna had worn sixty years and eighty pounds earlier, on the day she married her dear departed husband, Alonzo.

Everyone said that Lisa looked radiant that day. Rafe himself thought she had never looked more beautiful. It seemed as if a weight had been lifted—and indeed it had—

and its absence had made her stand taller, prouder, as she held the hand of the man she loved and promised her heart to him forever.

Rafe, in turn, could not have been happier as he offered his vow to her:

"I've made a lot of mistakes in my years," he said. "And one of the worst was when I was stupid enough to let you go back in college. I won't make that mistake again, Leese." He paused. "I don't know whether it was fate or just good luck that brought us back together, but thank God that it did. Because you are my heart. You beat inside me every moment of every day. And from this day forward I will love you, cherish you and do everything in my power to protect you and our beautiful daughter."

By the time he was finished, they both had tears in their eyes.

And the kiss that followed was exquisite.

AFTER THE SHOOTING at Sloan's house, Rafe, the other Francos and their rogue operation had been roundly condemned by the police and the press alike.

Until, that is, the data chip was revealed.

When all the guards had been neutralized and an ambulance was called for Sloan—

although resuscitation was a moot point by then—Kate conducted a search of Sloan's study and found a data chip in one of his desk drawers.

Plugging it into her phone, she quickly discovered that it was indeed the one taken from the bank, complete with promised names, dates and bribe amounts that exposed Sloan's entire network of sycophants, including some of the very people who had condemned the Francos.

But once the information came to light, the dominoes began to fall. The first to cave was Lola Berletti, Sloan's attorney, who volunteered to tell all in exchange for immunity. With her statement, Rafe was exonerated and the charges against him were dropped.

Kate and the organized crime unit were tasked with the arrests of five judges, fourteen police officers, two city council members and an FBI agent who had been in Sloan's pocket for nearly fifteen years.

When the dust had cleared, Rafe did what he should have done three years ago in college. Because he'd known even then, despite their miscommunication, that he wanted his relationship with Lisa to last forever. And ever.

And ever.

So he asked her to marry him.

Now, standing here, exchanging vows with the woman he loved, in front of the *family* he loved, was a moment he would never forget.

But the highlight of the day was little Chloe.

Rafe's daughter had not only been the picture of perfection serving as flower girl for the occasion, but also she, with the help of Beatrice, had been in charge of decorating, as well.

And taped to the back of every folding chair lined up in Grandma's Natalie's backyard, were her carefully colored pictures.

Of pink and blue kitty cats.

* * * * *

LARGER-PRINT BOOKS!
GET 2 FREE LARGER-PRINT NOVELS PLUS
2 FREE GIFTS!

◆HARLEQUIN®

INTRIGUE®

BREATHTAKING ROMANTIC SUSPENSE

YES! Please send me 2 FREE LARGER-PRINT Harlequin Intrigue® novels and my 2 FREE gifts (gifts are worth about $10). After receiving them, if I don't wish to receive any more books, I can return the shipping statement marked "cancel." If I don't cancel, I will receive 6 brand-new novels every month and be billed just $5.24 per book in the U.S. or $5.99 per book in Canada. That's a saving of at least 13% off the cover price! It's quite a bargain! Shipping and handling is just 50¢ per book in the U.S. and 75¢ per book in Canada.* I understand that accepting the 2 free books and gifts places me under no obligation to buy anything. I can always return a shipment and cancel at any time. Even if I never buy another book, the two free books and gifts are mine to keep forever.

199/399 HDN FVQ7

Name	(PLEASE PRINT)	

Address		Apt. #

City	State/Prov.	Zip/Postal Code

Signature (if under 18, a parent or guardian must sign)

Mail to the **Harlequin® Reader Service:**
IN U.S.A.: P.O. Box 1867, Buffalo, NY 14240-1867
IN CANADA: P.O. Box 609, Fort Erie, Ontario L2A 5X3

Are you a subscriber to Harlequin Intrigue books
and want to receive the larger-print edition?
Call 1-800-873-8635 today or visit www.ReaderService.com.

* Terms and prices subject to change without notice. Prices do not include applicable taxes. Sales tax applicable in N.Y. Canadian residents will be charged applicable taxes. Offer not valid in Quebec. This offer is limited to one order per household. Not valid for current subscribers to Harlequin Intrigue Larger-Print books. All orders subject to credit approval. Credit or debit balances in a customer's account(s) may be offset by any other outstanding balance owed by or to the customer. Please allow 4 to 6 weeks for delivery. Offer available while quantities last.

Your Privacy—The Harlequin® Reader Service is committed to protecting your privacy. Our Privacy Policy is available online at www.ReaderService.com or upon request from the Harlequin Reader Service.

We make a portion of our mailing list available to reputable third parties that offer products we believe may interest you. If you prefer that we not exchange your name with third parties, or if you wish to clarify or modify your communication preferences, please visit us at www.ReaderService.com/consumerschoice or write to us at Harlequin Reader Service Preference Service, P.O. Box 9062, Buffalo, NY 14269. Include your complete name and address.

HILP13

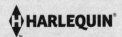

REQUEST YOUR FREE BOOKS!

2 FREE NOVELS
PLUS 2 FREE GIFTS!

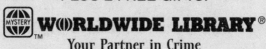

WORLDWIDE LIBRARY®

Your Partner in Crime

YES! Please send me 2 FREE novels from the Worldwide Library® series and my 2 FREE gifts (gifts are worth about $10). After receiving them, if I don't wish to receive any more books, I can return the shipping statement marked "cancel." If I don't cancel, I will receive 4 brand-new novels every month and be billed just $5.24 per book in the U.S. or $6.24 per book in Canada. That's a savings of at least 34% off the cover price. It's quite a bargain! Shipping and handling is just 50¢ per book in the U.S. and 75¢ per book in Canada.* I understand that accepting the 2 free books and gifts places me under no obligation to buy anything. I can always return a shipment and cancel at any time. Even if I never buy another book, the two free books and gifts are mine to keep forever.

414/424 WDN FVUV

Name	(PLEASE PRINT)	
Address		Apt. #
City	State/Prov.	Zip/Postal Code

Signature (if under 18, a parent or guardian must sign)

Mail to the **Harlequin® Reader Service:**
IN U.S.A.: P.O. Box 1867, Buffalo, NY 14240-1867
IN CANADA: P.O. Box 609, Fort Erie, Ontario L2A 5X3

Want to try two free books from another line?
Call 1-800-873-8635 or visit www.ReaderService.com.

* Terms and prices subject to change without notice. Prices do not include applicable taxes. Sales tax applicable in N.Y. Canadian residents will be charged applicable taxes. Offer not valid in Quebec. This offer is limited to one order per household. Not valid for current subscribers to the Worldwide Library series. All orders subject to credit approval. Credit or debit balances in a customer's account(s) may be offset by any other outstanding balance owed by or to the customer. Please allow 4 to 6 weeks for delivery. Offer available while quantities last.

Your Privacy—The Harlequin® Reader Service is committed to protecting your privacy. Our Privacy Policy is available online at www.ReaderService.com or upon request from the Harlequin Reader Service.

We make a portion of our mailing list available to reputable third parties that offer products we believe may interest you. If you prefer that we not exchange your name with third parties, or if you wish to clarify or modify your communication preferences, please visit us at www.ReaderService.com/consumerschoice or write to us at Harlequin Reader Service Preference Service, P.O. Box 9062, Buffalo, NY 14269. Include your complete name and address.

WWL13